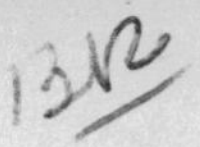

Abigail is stunned to discover her rescuer is none other than the despised Lord Sutton.

Remembering her manners, she curtsied reflexively despite the fact that such a vile man deserved no respect.

She looked back up onto his countenance. So this was the man Father wanted her to marry! The man who stopped to speak to her the night she was writing in her diary. The man who charged her with the phrase "peppery." Indeed!

She opened her mouth to admonish him, but his searching eyes, filled with wonder and kindness, stopped her.

Her anger evaporated. Rather than feeling threatened, a sense of safety and security took hold of her. Somehow, she knew that as long as she trusted this man, he would protect her. Yet Lord Sutton was a known rake and gambler. Perhaps this was his stock in trade, to deceive innocent women. Flashing blue eyes, a straight nose, and wavy ebony hair would be enough to draw the attention of any woman, enough to lure an innocent into thinking he loved her, only to leave her alone and abandoned, her heart broken.

Father in heaven, do not let me succumb to his lies!

Abigail felt a sense of peace. She observed the face of her host. Anyone could see that he was outwardly handsome. Honing in on his eyes, Abigail wondered about the state of his soul. When she studied his face, she could feel emanating from him a sense of peace, a peace she found only in those persons in whom the Lord dwelt. Instinctively, she felt that he belonged to the Lord Jesus Christ. But how could that be? Could the rumors whispered in local drawing rooms be wrong?

TAMELA HANCOCK MURRAY shares her home in Virginia with her godly husband and their two beautiful daughters. The car is her second home as she chauffeurs her girls to their many activities related to church, school, sports, scouting, and music. She is thankful that several local Christian radio stations allow her family to spend much of their driving time in praise and worship. Tamela hopes that her stories of God-centered romance edify and entertain her sisters in Christ.

Books By Tamela Hancock Murray

HEARTSONG PRESENTS

HP213—Picture of Love
HP408—Destinations
HP453—The Elusive Mr. Perfect
HP501—Thrill of the Hunt

A Light among Shadows

Tamela Hancock Murray

Heartsong Presents

A note from the author:
I love to hear from my readers! You may correspond with me by writing:

Tamela Hancock Murray
Author Relations
PO Box 719
Uhrichsville, OH 44683

ISBN 1-58660-772-3

A LIGHT AMONG SHADOWS

PRINTED IN THE U.S.A.

one

"Abigail Pettigrew! Get in this house right now or you'll catch your death of cold!" Griselda Pettigrew's shrill voice, calling from the verandah, cut through the autumn twilight.

Sitting with her back against a great oak with shriveled brown leaves still clinging to its branches, Abigail looked up from writing in her diary. "Yes, Mother," she shouted. Abigail tried not to wrinkle her nose when she used the familiar name.

Obviously satisfied that Abigail would obey, Griselda shut the heavy front door behind her. As soon as the woman's soot black curls disappeared from view, Abigail stuck out her tongue. The gesture gave her a sense of satisfaction even though her stepmother couldn't see it.

Once Abigail's dearest Mama had been taken home to the Lord after a prolonged illness, Griselda had wasted no time in becoming the second Mrs. George Pettigrew. As soon as Father's new bride had set foot on the estate, she'd insisted Abigail call her "Mother." Never mind that Griselda had been brought into the world only a decade earlier than her new stepdaughter.

When Abigail had protested to her father that she'd prefer to call Griselda by her first name, he'd dismissed her wishes. "Better to make your new stepmother feel welcome in our home, Abigail. As high-spirited as you are, she'll have her hands full teaching you to be a proper lady." Then he'd chuckled.

As his head moved with the rhythm of his laughter, Abigail had noticed how his graying hair shone in the light of the oil lantern. Not so long ago, his hair had been a burnished brown, so deep in color that it appeared almost black. Since he had wed Griselda, gray hairs had appeared with increasing frequency.

"My Griselda will earn the right to be called your mother before all is said and done," Father had admonished her.

As she sat remembering the determination that had filled his words, Abigail quivered with anger.

"No, she won't! Never!" Abigail muttered, banging the diary against her bent knees. An angry breath filled the air in front of her, forming a thick whiff of steam that quickly dissipated against the frigid temperature.

"My, but are we not peppery on this fine evening!"

Abigail gave a start at the sound of a horse's whinny. A stranger had stopped in front of her, a fine figure of a man perched high upon an ebony steed. Since night was falling in haste, Abigail could barely make out his straight nose and smiling lips. Blue eyes bored through her as a steel hook pierces the mouth of a fish. Though she felt as stunned as a captured trout, somehow she knew if this stranger were the fisherman who caught her, she would not object.

The way he unabashedly studied her, Abigail could see that her captor sought to prolong the sport. "And are we not bold on this fine evening, Sir?"

"Perhaps," he said with a hearty laugh. "Are you the lady of this estate?"

"I am the daughter."

His eyes fixed their gaze upon her face. "Then I must warn you not to linger in such close proximity to the road. You wouldn't want to be taken away." With another laugh and a "Giddyap, Midnight!" the stranger galloped away.

"Indeed!" she huffed, though by that time he had ventured too far away to hear. "Who is he to tell me what to do? Yet I wonder why he hurries so?" She rose from her spot. At that moment, she realized the seat of her green dress had become moist from the damp ground. A tickle in her throat caused her to cough. "Maybe Griselda was right to call me in. But I shall never concede such a thing to her!"

She clutched the diary inside the crook of her arm, against her chest, and secured in her fist the quill and sealed bottle of ink. Shivering, Abigail used her free hand to wrap her cotton shawl around her shoulders. With a quick pace, she headed toward the house. As she passed the kitchen, which occupied a small building separate from the main house, the rich smell of roasted mutton and freshly baked bread enveloped her nostrils. Her writing had been interrupted, but at least Mattie's delicious meal would be her reward.

Abigail remembered the times she'd helped Mattie churn butter and create delectable cakes. But those times were to be no more. "You're a Pettigrew, not a cook," Griselda reminded her. "I know your mama was too ill these past years to train you properly. I shall teach you to oversee the operations of the home, not to engage in work that is far below your station."

"But Mother, I like churning butter. And on chilly days the kitchen fire beckons me with its warmth."

"The kitchen fire, indeed! What is the matter with you, Abigail? You are to the manor born, not the prodigy of a scullery maid and a stable hand. Many other girls would gladly give up their families to be in your position."

"Then perhaps I shall exchange places with one of them." Abigail's rash statement wasn't sincere, but the shocked look on Griselda's face had been worthy compensation.

Abigail focused her attention on the present. She was careful to shut the front door slowly so it wouldn't creak as she entered. She wanted to deposit her diary in her bedchamber before dinner, away from Griselda's prying eyes. Pleased that she wasn't spotted in the foyer, Abigail slipped up the winding mahogany staircase. Her slim figure easily navigated the steps without causing a sound. Hastening to the second door on the right of the hallway, she stole into her bedchamber and fastened the heavy wood door behind her. Once safely inside, she let out a contented sigh. She would have a few moments alone with the thoughts she had recorded in the little leather-bound book before the gong sounded to summon her to appear at the dinner table.

Cold cinders in the fireplace offered no relief from the chill.

Funny, but not long ago, the servants never would have let the fire go out so early. Abigail kept her shawl about her shoulders. She made a straight course for the bed but stopped short when she remembered her moist dress. Abigail ran a hand over the back and discovered to her dismay that her dress held the damp. Sighing, she plopped down on the rug beside her bed. If she stained her quilt, a lecture was sure to follow.

Abigail forgot how the rug offered little cushion against the hard floor as she opened her diary and read:

October 29, 1819

Dear Diary,

Today was most spectacular! Henry—handsome Henry—spotted me picking apples in our orchard. He stopped to inquire after my health. Any gentleman would have done the same, certainly, but I know Henry is considering me as a prospective wife. You ask, Dear Diary, "How can you tell?" Because he looks me up and down—oh, the thought is enough to make me blush! And when he does, his eyes sparkle with interest. Much interest. I do wonder when he will inquire of Father about courting me? Oh, to be Lady Hanover! The thought is too pleasing to bear!

Abigail let her gaze wander to the bright green ceiling. To be the lady of Hanover Manor! With Henry by her side, nothing could make her happier. Her Henry wasn't so impudent as that strange man who galloped by, calling her—what was it? Peppery? Peppery!

"Well, I never!" she muttered.

Abigail picked up her quill and dipped it in ink. She had an addition to make to the day's entry.

A most appalling man stopped and spoke to me today, Dear Diary. Eyeing me as I sat beside our favorite oak, he had the nerve to call me peppery! Peppery! I've never been so insulted in all my twenty years!

When I challenged him, he laughed and then galloped off as though the whole of England were afire and he was the one who had to save her! Dear Diary, I hope I never see the likes of him again—even if he does have eyes bluer than the bluest sky.

❧

Tedric Sutton galloped toward his family estate. So the girl he had just met was none other than Abigail Pettigrew. He had heard only small tidbits about her from his brother. Tedric recalled Cecil's description. Abigail was young and untried in the ways of the world, Cecil had informed him, his voice scoffing with each turn of phrase. Knowing that Cecil intended to take the Pettigrew girl to be his wife, Tedric cringed. If not for her esteemed family name, Abigail would never have gained Cecil's notice.

No wonder Tedric had been astonished to discover his future sister-in-law was so, so—peppery. A smile tickled his lips. She certainly had been indignant at the description. His brother would have his hands full keeping her reined in at the estate.

Tedric recalled the fiery young woman. She glowed with beauty, the type of unaffected loveliness he hadn't seen among the sophisticated ladies of his acquaintance in London society. They were experienced at batting their eyelashes and using smooth words to flatter men. Even though he was the second son and not heir to the estate, Tedric never lacked for their companionship when he attended social gatherings in the city. He recalled the last party he'd attended. A flock of women took notice of him. Why, in their eagerness, did they seem jaded?

They were nothing like Abigail. From their short encounter, he'd developed the distinct impression that Abigail believed in the power of romantic love. He somehow knew she wanted to be swept off her tiny feet into the protective arms of a man she could lavish her affections upon forevermore.

He felt his smile fade. His brother was not that person. Nor would Cecil ever be that man. Not for Abigail, not for anyone. Cecil didn't know how to cherish a woman. His idea of marriage was to make a successful match with the most beautiful and wealthy woman available, a woman who would look the other way as he wasted money on games of chance. In return, she would live at the impressive Sutton estate. She would bear the highly regarded Sutton name, as would her children. The match Cecil wanted would be considered successful in worldly terms, not spiritual. Tedric wondered if his brother had a spiritual bone in his body.

"Father in heaven, forgive me," he muttered. "I am not my brother's judge, nor any man's judge. Yet I know my own brother all too well. Lord, change Cecil's heart, for Abigail's sake."

By the time Midnight turned into the road leading to the front lawn of the Sutton estate, Tedric's mood was pensive. The betrothal between Cecil and Abigail was already arranged. He couldn't protect Abigail. His only power lay in being the best brother-in-law he could be. A feeble role, to be sure. But one he was determined to mine for all its abundance.

❧

"Abigail!" Griselda shouted from the bottom of the stairs, interrupting her dreams. "Come to dinner this instant!"

The girl shook her head in wonder. Griselda only shouted like that when Abigail missed the sound of the gong. Apparently, her writing had immersed her in another world and left her oblivious to that earlier summons to dinner. "Yes, Mother," she called in answer.

Sighing, Abigail secured her quill and ink on her nightstand and slipped her diary underneath her mattress. She poured fresh water from the white pitcher into the basin on her cherry wood dresser and washed and dried her hands and face well enough to pass Griselda's inspection. As she took to the stairs, Abigail didn't mind if a couple of the boards creaked. Once Griselda called, each moment was of the essence.

"What was the cause of your delay?" Griselda queried when

she saw Abigail enter the dining room.

"I apologize, Mother. My toilette before dinner took longer than I anticipated." Seating herself, Abigail concentrated her gaze upon her plate.

"That is but a feeble excuse," Griselda said. "A proper lady is always prompt."

"Yes, Mother." Abigail's eyes remained downcast and focused on the intricate pattern of roses painted on the plate.

"There now. I think our mutton will still be hot enough, regardless of my daughter's tardiness." George Pettigrew's voice was kind. "Let us have our blessing." After uttering a word of thanks to the Lord for His bountiful provision, Abigail's father waited for the meal to be served.

As soon as the servant had performed her duties and exited the dining room, Griselda flipped her ivory-colored, linen napkin open and set it upon her lap. "Do you see this table? How well it is set? The food that is cooked and served to perfection? Do you see, Abigail?" Griselda swept a woolen-clad arm over the table.

"Yes, Mother." Abigail unfolded her napkin. Laying it over her knees, she noticed a seam had become frayed.

"Managing the meals is but one of the duties of a lady. Why, if I did not make it my business to watch the comings and goings in the kitchen, the cook would throw away half the food, let it spoil, or give away all our leftovers to her ne'er-do-well relations. And the chambermaid would be flirting with the deliverymen and the stable boys instead of performing her duties. Without me, this manor would be in perpetual disorder, just as it was when I first arrived."

"You have performed superbly, my darling," Abigail's father said to his wife.

"I seek not praise, but to try to make your daughter see what she must learn as a lady of her station." Griselda's thin lips turned downward. Her eyes took on a chilly cast. "Unfortunately, her appearance will not entice any suitors. She looks too much like her departed mama. Hopeless hair. Brown eyes that are too big for the rest of her face." Her look of appraisal traveled to Abigail's bodice. "And I have abandoned all hope that her spindly figure will ever fill out properly."

Abigail willed herself to keep from crossing her arms over her chest.

Griselda looked down her long nose at Abigail's face. "At least your skin is unblemished."

"And so was Mama's. Her skin was the most beautiful I ever seen. And Mama had a sweet disposition too. Did she not, Father?" Abigail couldn't resist asking.

"That will be enough, Abigail." Father's voice was firm. "Griselda is only doing her best to teach you what shall be expected of you once you become a wife and mistress of your own estate. That is her duty to you and to me." Still, Abigail felt mollified to see him cast a warning look Griselda's way.

Griselda lifted her overloaded spoon halfway to her thin lips. "So what business did the earl of Sutton have with you, Abigail?"

Abigail stopped her fork in midair. "The earl of Sutton?"

"Yes. I saw you speaking with him just before you came inside." Griselda's tone indicated her disapproval.

Taken aback by the unexpected inquisition, Abigail stalled. "The light was so dim I could barely see him myself. How could you tell from so far away the man was Lord Sutton?"

"I could see by his black horse," Griselda answered. "Are you not aware that the Suttons are renowned for breeding horses with coats the color of midnight?"

"I suppose I had not contemplated such." Abigail remembered the name the man had called his horse. Midnight.

"You never contemplate anything of consequence," Griselda opined. "You spend too much time writing in that book of yours, daydreaming instead of learning how best to oversee the daily operations of a manor house. If you want to be a fine lady, these things you must learn. And learn well."

To Abigail's surprise, Father rose to her defense. "But surely the child is entitled to a bit of leisure. And if she uses her time to practice writing, all the better. Perfect penmanship is of great value to a lady."

"As if anyone can tell whether her penmanship is perfect or as irregular as the scratching of a hen. No one is allowed to read that diary but she." Griselda's stare bored into her step-daughter. "I wonder what she writes in it?"

Abigail's only answer was to take a delicate sip of hot tea.

"She is but a child." Father shrugged.

"I beg to differ. I was betrothed when I was her age."

From the corner of her eye, Abigail saw her father pat his wife upon the hand. "Now, now, Griselda, my darling. Your worry is needless. Did I not tell you I have plans for my little pet?"

Abigail returned her cup to its saucer and looked at her father. She could feel the rapid beating of her heart.

What plans could he possibly have for me?

two

"Plans? You have plans for me?" Abigail knew her shrill tone betrayed her shock.

Father smiled. The look of kindness in his eyes comforted Abigail. "As a matter of fact, I do," he said. "And they involve the earl himself." He leaned closer to her and paused as was his habit when conveying important news. "Abigail, you are betrothed to the earl of Sutton."

Betrothed to that awful man who called me peppery? But I do not love him! I love Henry Hanover! Please, I beg you, no!

As much as Abigail wanted to shout these words to her father, they remained stuck in her throat.

A self-satisfied smile took over Father's features as he tilted back into his chair, settling himself into it. He passed the linen napkin over his mouth, even though no food was evident upon it. "By this time next year, you will be the lady of Sutton Manor."

Her stepmother gasped. Abigail looked over to see that Griselda had stopped chewing. The shocked expression on her face seemed as frozen as January ice on a pond. At that moment, Abigail realized her own mouth hung open, yet she remained mute.

"Betrothed? When did this happen?" Griselda asked.

"The arrangement became official two days ago, when I received his reply from London."

"London? He lives in London?" Abigail asked.

"If you are worried that your marriage will require you to move to the city, never fear. As I said, you will be the lady of Sutton Manor. Perhaps you might live part of the year in London, but most of the time, you shall be at home, managing the estate."

Abigail recalled Sutton Manor, a place she had visited only once, for a long-ago Christmas party. Lady Elizabeth had been in her prime and a popular hostess. A few years later, illness rendered her an invalid. In his grief, her husband became a recluse until his death only a few months ago. Abigail supposed his demise was the reason his eldest son, who had inherited the title and property, had returned from gallivanting in London.

Not that she blamed the young earl for abandoning the house. The hideous monstrosity, with gables, columns, and gargoyles on all four wings, was an anathema. She shuddered. "But what if I do not wish to manage the Sutton estate?"

"Don't be a fool, you silly goose," Griselda snapped, her sharp tongue seeming to have suffered no ill effects from the shock. "Your father has ensured a clever match. Much more clever than I ever would have expected for you." She turned to her husband. "Well done, my dear."

"Well done?" Abigail nearly spit the words. "You betrothed me to a man I know not in the slightest without even asking me? And you call that well done?" Her stomach lurched with a combination of fear and anger. She clutched at the material of her dress.

"Indeed I do." Father leaned close again. His mouth was pursed into a thin line, an expression that meant he would brook no opposition. "This marriage will compound the fortunes of both our families. Our power and wealth will be multiplied several times over."

"But you never cared about your fortune before. The Lord has always blessed us with more than enough."

"Circumstances can change," Griselda answered.

Abigail narrowed her eyes at her stepmother. "Indeed."

Father cleared his throat. "The war with France has made times more difficult for all of us. But even if the Suttons had not a pence, their good name would be a marvelous branch on the Pettigrew family tree."

"Then you must be deaf to the rumors surrounding the earl," Abigail observed. "He is a known gambler and rake.

I wonder if he agreed to marry me only to secure himself more funds for his idle pleasures!"

"That is enough, Abigail," Father lashed back. "You will not speak to me in such a disrespectful manner."

"I beg your indulgence," Abigail apologized, though she didn't mean it in her heart. She had a feeling if she tarried over dinner, she would blurt out something truly regrettable. She bunched her napkin in the fingers of both hands. Anxiety had made them tense. "May I be excused from the table?"

"But you have barely touched your mutton," Griselda objected. "To waste is never wise."

Abigail swallowed. Her stomach felt as though it had tied itself into one large knot. She couldn't imagine burdening it with another bite of food, so she shook her head.

"Very well. You may be excused," Father muttered.

"And do not ask for more food later!" Griselda warned.

Abigail nodded before she ran to her bedchamber. She had to escape the fate her father had in mind for her. She had to do something. And soon.

❧

"Honour thy father and thy mother: that thy days may be long upon the land which the Lord thy God giveth thee."

As she sat on her bed, Abigail stared at Exodus 20:12. She had been referring to that verse often as of late. Reading God's commandment forced her to face the reality that since Father had married Griselda, Abigail's life had become increasingly difficult. Unwanted tears burned her eyes and wet her cheeks. She swiped at them with the back of her hands, but the motions only served to quell the tide a portion. Abigail moved her Bible so the pages wouldn't become stained with tears.

Heavenly Father, how can I honor such a selfish parent? I know I cannot expect Griselda to be as sweet as my own mama, but why has Father abandoned me? Why has he developed a desire to increase his fortune?

Abigail surmised she already knew the answer. Despite

Griselda's admonitions against waste, she didn't seem averse to spending money on whatever she pleased. Griselda hosted lavish parties for her friends. She enjoyed a stream of invited houseguests who thought nothing of enjoying the Pettigrews' hospitality for a fortnight at a time. Griselda made certain to purchase a new gown and adornments for every occasion, along with fresh morning and afternoon dresses each season. She took quarterly journeys to Bath. Abigail didn't wonder why the family coffers were low.

As much as she desired to be a good daughter, Abigail couldn't sacrifice everything for the benefit of her stepmother's idle pursuits. At the moment, she couldn't even imagine speaking to the woman in a civil manner. Her only option was to remain in her bedchamber for the rest of the evening. Perhaps the situation would appear less wretched after a night's slumber.

She drew a heavy nightdress out of a drawer and put it on over her head. The white fabric was chilly from being stored in a cold room. Seeking comfort, she pulled the two steps out from under her high bed and climbed up so she could snuggle in the mountain of blankets and quilts that clothed her mattress on these frigid nights. Soon the heat from her body warmed the sheets, and she drifted into a fitful sleep.

The next morning, Abigail awoke before breakfast. For an instant, she felt free. Then she recalled the announcement from the previous evening. A ship's anchor couldn't have done more to weigh her down. "Oh, why could not Father have betrothed me to Henry Hanover? Surely his name is as fine, and his holdings seem comparable." Her sigh was audible.

She paused for a moment. "Why, that is it! The solution to my problem!"

Abigail bounded out of bed and lit the candle on her nightstand. She headed for the top drawer of her bureau, where she kept a few pages of simple white linen writing paper. She gathered one sheet and an envelope, along with her quill and ink. Since her bedchamber housed no desk, she used the even surface of the nightstand's cherry wood as a temporary writing surface. Sitting on the side of the bed, legs hanging, she leaned over the paper and began to write:

Dear Henry,

I must see you right away on an urgent matter. Please meet me in the back garden by the rose bushes just before dusk this evening.

Yours,
Abigail Pettigrew

Abigail folded the note. Hands shaking, she used the flaming candle to melt a bit of crimson wax for sealing it. Excited, she hurried to the wardrobe and selected a blue morning dress whose deep pockets would serve to conceal the missive. Later, she would be able to slip the message to Luke, a stable boy she could trust to make such deliveries to the Hanover estate in secret.

Moments later, Abigail's heart beat rapidly as she consumed her sausage and eggs. Keeping quiet seemed the best way not to reveal her hidden thoughts.

"You seem in a much more subdued mood this fine morning," Griselda observed. "I hope that means you have accepted the betrothal."

Abigail didn't respond, hoping her continued silence would be construed as acquiescence.

"Of course she has," Father answered for her. "Abigail is a good daughter."

"Good." Griselda snapped open her napkin, causing a muted crackle to fill the air. "Since the earl has obviously returned from London, I suggest we plan a betrothal party. Naturally, we shall invite. . ."

Abigail allowed Griselda's recitation of her guest list and other plans to wash over her without committing them to memory. There would be no party. Not if she and Henry had anything to say about it.

❧

As twilight neared, Abigail slipped out of doors. She breathed a sigh of relief when no one tried to stop her. If her stepmother thought Abigail planned to write in her diary, she would make sure to find work that would necessitate her immediate return to the house.

Griselda had often expressed how much she hated the time Abigail spent with her diary. While the given reason for this aversion was that the entries took Abigail away from her duties, Abigail surmised that Griselda also feared her entries contained unflattering descriptions of her stepmother.

Abigail grinned to herself. As if she would waste precious ink on Griselda! Abigail recorded her thoughts about much more important events and people. People such as Henry Hanover.

She sat on the bench by the rose bushes, which were devoid of blooms since winter was nigh. For Griselda's benefit, she opened her diary and then dipped her quill in ink. She might as well write about her feelings as she waited for her beloved. Yet when she set quill to parchment, no words flowed. Her mind always went blank in moments of high anticipation, and this time was no exception.

She tried not to look up too often as she waited. She saw no need to tip off any of Griselda's favorite servants that she might be involved in some intrigue. Desperate to appear innocent, Abigail scribbled drawings of the roses she wished were in bloom.

As dark deepened, she tapped her foot. Why was Henry late? Luke had assured her that he had delivered the message and kept his errand a secret. Her heart seemed to jump in her throat. Maybe Henry wouldn't show at all! No. He wouldn't treat her that way. Not her Henry.

As though her thoughts caused him to materialize, at that moment she heard the sound of a galloping horse. She looked up to see Henry. Abigail let out a sigh of relief as she watched him dismount.

In spite of her best intentions not to look eager, she ran to his side.

"Henry."

"Abigail." His knowing smile made her want to draw him closer. Sudden shyness and respect for propriety kept her feet rooted in place.

"I–I hope you do not think me too forward. You know it is not my habit to write such messages to men as the one I sent to you today."

"Of course not. I know you never would have written had the matter not been urgent, as you said it was in your letter." A worried look touched his face. "Why did you want to see me? Are you in some sort of trouble?"

"Yes." She shook her head. "I mean, no."

His expression turned indulgent. "Is it yes or no?"

"I am in great distress, through no fault of my own. Father just informed me that he has betrothed me to the earl of Sutton." She averted her eyes, studying her clenched hands. "I cannot marry him."

"I see." Henry mulled over her words, as though absorbing the shock. "But if your father has promised, then your family's reputation will be questioned if you disobey."

"It is not my desire to disobey, but—" She let out an aggrieved breath. Why were men so obtuse? "I cannot marry him." Abigail lifted her eyes to meet Henry's stare, hoping the distress her gaze must reveal would move him. "What must I do?"

"Marry someone else, of course." His cavalier answer, accompanied by a small shrug, stabbed her no less than a genuine dagger.

"Someone else." Abigail paused for effect.

"Yes." He patted his horse as though he were a spectator, not a participant, in a conversation that would determine the direction of his future—and hers.

She cleared her throat. "You seem to think that would be easy enough."

"Of course."

He surveyed her, his bold look beginning at the top of her head. Henry's assessment of her form ended with the tips of the shoes that peeked from underneath the hem of her dress. Abigail felt uncomfortable, but if Henry were to become her husband, and soon, she supposed he could enjoy certain privileges denied to other men.

"Surely a young woman of your beauty and proud family name has many suitors?" he ventured.

Though his inspection had yielded a compliment, Abigail bowed her head. "Mama was ill so many years. My life revolved around her. When she passed on, I, of course, went into mourning."

He nodded. "I remember. Your life has not been one of frivolity."

"I suppose that is why Father thought it best to find a husband for me. He never asked me whom I might like. He did not inquire if there is any man I might consider or if there is anyone I have admired for years." Abigail dared not look up, lest she witness Henry's scorn. Or worse, laughter.

"Are you saying. . . ?"

Abigail looked into his face.

His eyes widened as his mouth slackened. "Are you suggesting—me?" His tone showed he was not insulted.

"A lady should not be so bold." Abigail once more stared at her hands.

"And a man should not be such a milksop as to turn a blind eye to such charm."

Heart seeming to beat out of her chest, Abigail lifted her gaze to his. "I wish not to be forward."

"Indeed you are not." He ogled her face, then her figure. "Although I will need time."

"Time is the one commodity we have not. If we are to go through with this, it must happen. Tonight."

"Tonight? Oh!"

Something about his voice made Abigail cringe. She

ignored her sudden wave of uncertainty. "Tonight."

He stood to his full height and raised his forefinger to the sky. "Then tonight it shall be. I shall bring my carriage around to the churchyard as the clock strikes eleven hours."

"You will?" Her voice displayed the mixture of surprise and glee she felt.

"So I shall. Tomorrow morning, Abigail Pettigrew, you shall be my wife."

three

"My, but the air has grown chilly tonight," Griselda commented after dinner. She sent Father a look that beckoned him to add a log to the fire, but he rattled his paper, unmoved.

Abigail chose not to comment. The weather was the last thing on her mind. Tonight was the night she would meet her beloved! Henry, the man she had desired ever since they met at Lord Windsor's homecoming so many years ago, would at last become her own. How bleak her life had been until the day she saw Henry for the first time. He had been escorting a rather plain heiress, but Henry had noticed Abigail among the crowd and, with a wink and knowing smile, had seemed to read her mind and soul.

She remembered Father's displeasure. How dare a man be so forward when they had not been properly introduced! But what did Father know? He had courted Mother so long ago, and Griselda—well!

Abigail shivered with a mixture of disgust and not a little bit of cold, now that Griselda mentioned it. Throughout dinner, Abigail had felt comfortable. A flickering fire in the dining room had provided warmth as they feasted on roast beef. For once she agreed with Griselda. Only an hour had passed since dinner's conclusion, but the house had already grown frosty.

She looked at the fire in the parlor where the three of them were gathered. Flames blazed and crackled, consuming several logs. The heavy scent of pine-tinged smoke wafted through the room. Yet she still felt cold. Abigail adjusted her lap quilt so that it covered as much of her body as possible. She snuggled into the golden brocaded fabric of the wing chair, the mate to the one in which her father sat nearby as he caught up on the news in the weekly paper. Griselda reclined upon a brocaded chaise lounge, involved in a work of fiction. Abigail picked up her needle to resume the mending Griselda had assigned her earlier.

"You are correct, my dear Griselda," Father remarked. "The temperature has fallen considerably since this afternoon. Winter must be greeting us with full force at last."

"Then I hope we have plenty of fuel to get us through the season. I do so hate to be chilled," Griselda said.

As Father gave his assurances, Abigail returned her unseeing gaze to the shirt she was mending. She was to meet Henry at eleven, an hour after she was supposed to be in bed. Since she would be forced to walk to the churchyard by herself, Abigail knew she would have to travel lightly. She'd already packed a dress and undergarments in a leather satchel that would be easy to carry the distance. Before she departed, Abigail planned to slip into the kitchen and add two slices of leftover roast beef and a good chunk of bread to her bag. Once that was accomplished, the contents of the satchel would be enough to see her through until she returned home with Henry by her side, triumphant in the victory of becoming his wife.

At least, she hoped she would be triumphant. Disobeying her father was not something she considered lightly. But what other choice did she have? Once he discovered her deception, Father was likely to be angry. She would have to face that. Yet she was certain Henry would prove to be a good husband. He would not spend the family fortune at gaming tables. Of that she was sure. It was only a matter of time before Father would see things her way. Maybe he would even bless her marriage. That was her fondest wish.

In the meantime, Abigail prayed to the Lord for His forgiveness. The transgression she was about to commit was serious. Still, she trusted in the Lord's love. In His mercy, He would understand what she was about to do, and why. As she sewed, she recalled Jesus' words that she had read that day during devotions: "Peace I leave with you, my peace I give unto you: not as the world giveth, give I unto you. Let not your heart be troubled, neither let it be afraid."

Abigail braced herself and tried not to be afraid. After all, Paul had been forgiven for persecuting Christians. He had gone on to become the apostle to the Gentiles. Surely the Lord could forgive her disobedience.

Putting her fears out of her mind, Abigail thought about what life would be like as Henry's wife. She had loved him from afar for so many years. No wonder he hadn't seemed amazed by her suggestion. Of course, Henry was taking a chance. Once their elopement was discovered, then he, too, would face her father's wrath. But together they would stand. Unshakable. Victorious. Married.

Once word about their marriage circulated, Abigail knew what the villagers would whisper. Henry's reputation would be called into question along with her own. But together, they could face any trial. After a few months, the rumors, speculations, and half-truths would quiet, and their story would become another entry in local folklore. She imagined that when she and Henry were old and gray, people would see their impromptu marriage for the romantic story it was.

"Look at them!" they would say. "Years ago, Lady Hanover confessed her love, and she married Lord Hanover in secret, in defiance of her father. He had planned for Lady Hanover to marry a scoundrel and a rake. Imagine that. But her love for Lord Hanover and his love for her conquered all. How romantic!"

Abigail pictured herself looking out upon the rolling hills of the Hanover estate. Despite Griselda's doubts, she would maintain the manor to perfection. Henry would be pleased.

She allowed her thoughts to wander to another grand house—Sutton Manor. The estate of her betrothed. Without her to look after that home, what would be its fate? Certainly the house would remain fine for a time, but as the years passed, the main house, the herb house, the kitchen, the smokehouse, the stables, the barns—everything—would fall into disrepair, each structure a victim of neglect.

"The Suttons were once the wealthiest among the local aristocracy," the villagers would say. "But the earl gambled away their fortune. What a shame!"

She thought of what the earl would look like decades into the future. He would be decrepit, gray, gnarled, and gout-ridden, and the light would have long since disappeared from his blue eyes. Abigail felt sorry for the elderly man she pictured. Then she remembered. . . .

She shuddered. With the sudden motion, Griselda looked upon her. Abigail shifted in her seat, hoping to deflect any comments from her stepmother. When Griselda returned to her reading, Abigail sighed inwardly and resumed her fantasies.

Why had she thought of the earl's blue eyes? The image of the strangely handsome gentleman, erect in his saddle, wouldn't leave her mind. Obviously the beau her father had chosen for her was no monster in appearance. But to marry a man of such low character—a gambler and a rogue? She couldn't.

The sound of a newspaper crinkling caused Abigail to wake from her daydream and look at her father.

"Time for bed," he announced.

Abigail wasn't tired, but she was in no mood to argue. After knotting the thread to secure a wayward button, she folded her father's shirt, readying it for the laundress the following day. Griselda snapped her book shut. Father folded his paper and set it beside the chair. Ordinary motions to bring to a close another day. Motions she would no longer witness. Now that the time to meet Henry was near, Abigail felt an unwelcome surge of nervousness tinged by a sadness in knowing this would be her last evening spent in the home of her childhood.

"Good night, Mother." Abigail made her way to her father's chair. She leaned over and kissed him on the forehead. "Good night, Father."

He gave her a wistful smile. "Good night, my little Abigail." Extending his hand, he took hers and gave her fingers a gentle squeeze.

Her answer was a quick nod. She turned away and headed up the stairs quickly, lest tears begin to fall. The moment of truth was upon her. In only a few hours, her life would be changed forever.

❧

An icy drizzle began to slice through the air as Abigail made her way down Pickett Road. Night had fallen in all its ebony glory. Thankfully, her eyes had adjusted enough so she could discern the path in the darkness. Without warning, the wind changed direction. Whereas before the moisture had fallen against the side of her hooded velvet cape, now the frigid droplets smashed her full in the face, prickling before they melted against her soft flesh. Shivering, she pulled the cape closely around her. She wished she had worn a more substantial coat instead of giving in to vanity. The black velvet cape looked dramatic but offered only the slightest protection against freezing rain.

As soon as she had walked a few more yards along the small dirt road, Abigail would find herself at the local church. The agreed-upon meeting place. On Sundays when she looked forward to worship, Abigail felt her journey to the building brought her closer to the Lord. Tonight, her errand was much different. Each step seemed to take her farther from Him. Suddenly, Abigail wished that she and Henry had agreed upon a different place to meet.

"Lord, forgive me," she muttered under her breath.

At that moment, she stepped into a puddle of mud. Dirty water saturated the kid leather slipper and silk stocking that offered her foot meager protection against the elements. At least she could change her other clothes later.

She patted her hip, looking for the satchel. There was none. She paused in midstep, letting out a gasp. How could she have forgotten it? Never mind. Henry could buy her fresh clothing on the morrow.

Abigail lifted her skirt, grateful that only the hem of her garment had suffered from the mishap, as evidenced by a thin line of water on its front. Discouraged from battling precipitation, she wanted to stop. But she couldn't. She had to keep going.

The designated meeting place was in sight. That knowledge gladdened her heart, if only for a moment. She looked expectantly for a carriage, one that would keep her warm and sheltered after her fight with the elements. There was none. She stared as far as her eyes could see. Henry was nowhere, not even riding on a lone horse.

Where could he be? She was not early. Indeed, she was closer to being tardy. He should have been there, waiting for her. Did he not realize the danger of her being out alone, walking along the desolate road so late at night? He should have been eager to protect her from the weather, if nothing else.

Anger turned to fear. What if he had been detained for a reason beyond his control? What if he had been taken ill? What if her father had discovered their plans? What if at this very moment, Father stood before Henry at the Hanover estate, threatening him?

She shook her head. No. That couldn't be. If her father had discovered their plans, someone would have been sent to retrieve her, even if only to allow Father to punish her upon her safe arrival home.

Abigail slowed her steps, no longer eager to set foot upon the churchyard. The stalwart structure, comprised of stone, seemed to be passing judgment from its sturdy perch. The double oak doors she passed through each Sunday seemed to be sealed—as though she would never again be permitted to enter. Even a grove of trees, the site of so many church socials, seemed to mock her. Unable to ease her guilt, she turned away, casting her eyes upon the dirt path.

Only moments before, she could fight her feeling of cold with thoughts of Henry. Now she was conscious of her discomfort. Through the stone gate and into the churchyard she stepped. Pale white stones on her right marked the resting places of long-deceased ancestors. She could almost feel their judgment as she imagined their souls looking downward from heaven.

Well, they would just have to judge her. She was not about to give up. She stood erect, proud to meet her new fiancé. The man who would soon be her husband.

"But what if that does not happen? What will I do if Henry decides not to meet me? How will I face Father?" Shame flooded her being. She didn't want to think about the consequences should her plans to marry in secret fail.

"What am I thinking? Of course Henry will meet me. He has just been detained." She looked at the church. "I know. I shall see if the vicar left the doors unlocked. I shall seek shelter there. And until Henry arrives for me, I shall pray."

At that moment, she heard a horse galloping toward her.

"Henry!" she called.

The man on the horse did not answer, but neither did he slow his approach.

"Henry?" Her voice quivered.

Still, no answer.

Panic seized her. The stranger had seen her. Why didn't he answer? Who was he? Was he a neighbor who would sully her reputation with word that he had seen her alone, obviously waiting for someone? Or was he a bandit with robbery in mind? Or worse?

Fear clenched its icy fingers around her heart. The stranger was approaching with lightning speed. She had to get away!

Abigail tried to move her feet, but they stayed frozen in place. Uncooperative, her knees weakened and then lost their capacity to hold her weight. They bent. Abigail knew she was falling. Her world was collapsing with her. She couldn't think. She couldn't breathe.

"Heavenly Father, please help me!"

At that moment, she lost consciousness, her mind shutting out the nightmare she had made of her life.

four

Tedric Sutton witnessed the caped figure falling to the ground in a faint. He stared in wonder.

"This must not be a bandit or troublemaker. But who?" He reined in his steed, leaped over the stone wall, and then rushed to the fallen body. The slight frame, cloaked in black velvet, obviously belonged to a woman.

"What possessed a woman to be out this late at night?" he wondered.

Her garment showed her to be a lady of means. But who could it be?

He placed his forefinger underneath her nostrils. Slight breaths warmed his flesh. Relieved that she lived, he lifted her cloaked head from the hard ground and held it in cupped hands. For the first time, he observed the woman's face. Lustrous dark blond curls surrounded pleasant features. Long lashes protruded from heavy, closed lids. Despite the cold, her lips were full and the color of roses.

He gasped. "The girl! This is the girl from the Pettigrew estate!" In spite of his reluctance to remain in the cold drizzle, he took a moment to drink in the beauty of her countenance. She looked so peaceful, as if in a deep, dreamless slumber.

A pang of guilt pierced his heart. "I must have frightened the poor thing out of her wits! Maybe that is why she fell." He drew her close to his chest in hopes of warming her frigid cheeks, reddened from harsh winter elements. Warm breath penetrated his coat and vest.

At that moment, he realized he shouldn't linger. He needed to take her safely home. And quickly, lest she catch her death.

As he lifted her full weight from the ground, he noted with amazement how light she felt. Just a slip of a girl. He continued to question her presence at the churchyard so late in the night.

"Dear Father in heaven," he prayed, "I have no thought as to why she is here, but I thank You for sending me here at this moment to provide this young lady with assistance." He shuddered at the thought of what could have happened if he had not appeared to rescue her.

Mounting his steed while holding a listless body, no matter how light, was difficult. All the same, he managed to place her awkwardly in front of him, holding on to her as if his very life depended upon her safety.

She stirred. "Henry?" She turned around, a little smile lighting her face. Eyes whose color he was unable to ascertain in the dark opened slightly. "Henry. You came for me."

Henry! The only Henry of his acquaintance was Henry Hanover. Tedric hoped Abigail hadn't come here to meet such a notorious rake. Henry's reputation was even worse than that of his own brother, the man to whom Abigail was betrothed. He swallowed. Was Abigail so desperate to get away from Cecil? Or had Henry, known for his smooth tongue, made promises too sweet for such an innocent to resist? Anger rose in his chest. Why, the next time he saw that cad, he would. . .

"Henry," she muttered.

Disappointment filled Tedric's being. "I shall take you home now," he whispered.

"Home? No!" She shook her head sleepily. "You promised. Please do not take me home. I never want to go back again. I want to be with you." Her lips puckered, and she tilted her head closer to his.

The temptation to seize the moment struck him mightily, but he resisted. He moved his head enough so her lips would miss his and urged her face to nestle on his shoulder. Clicking his tongue to signal his horse to trot, he headed in the only direction he could.

❧

Abigail awakened. Not wishing to depart from the pleasant state between dreamless slumber and total consciousness, she kept her eyes shut. The down pillow under her cheek offered her head a soft place to rest. Heavy blankets were cozy from the heat of her body. The air in the bedchamber was brisk, but that was to be expected since last night's fire had long since dissipated.

Already she dreaded the prospect of rising for the day. No doubt Griselda had made out a long list of tasks for her to do, ostensibly to train her to be the lady of her own manor one day. If only the work could wait until spring. Oh, how she hated winter! To keep warm, she would have to leap out of bed quickly and grab undergarments and a dress from the wardrobe. Frigid air enveloping her face suggested she would need to wear her heaviest wool. Letting out a soft groan, she threw the covers over her head. Maybe if she pretended to be asleep, Griselda would have mercy and delay her summons to breakfast and the day's tasks.

What day was it, anyway?

Inexplicably, her stomach felt as though it were leaping to her throat. Why?

She remembered. Last night she had been waiting to meet Henry, but he was late.

Henry!

Ignoring the chill, Abigail threw the covers off her head and sat upright.

Where was she?

The room she saw wasn't her own. Rather than a windowless cubby painted the color of greened copper, she had apparently spent the night in a magnificent chamber. She looked for her amateurishly carved cherry wardrobe. In its stead stood a large cabinet consisting of wood the color of strong black coffee. The wardrobe was decorated with intricate carvings, polished until they shone. The elaborate piece of furniture occupied a space between two large windows dressed in velvet. Beside the adjacent wall, a marble-topped nightstand housed a plain basin for her toilette. How peculiar that she didn't remember washing her face the previous evening. A stone fireplace bearing the remains of the preceding night's fire occupied most of the north wall. Abigail studied the wallpaper with its scenes of fox hunting.

Had she slept in a man's quarters?

A man's quarters! She drew the thick down covers up over her chest as though the masculine owner of the bedchamber were standing nearby, staring at her flesh clad only in a nightshift. A scratchy wool shift that didn't belong to her. How odd!

She noticed the covers. Attracted to the deep green color, she touched the fabric. The woven filaments felt soft yet durable. Silk? Green dyed silk? Surely she must be in a bedchamber of a fine home or inn.

Her thoughts returned to Henry. Henry! Her beloved Henry! The mere thought of him caused a warm glow to pass through her body. Had he spent a day's wages to provide her with a new nightshift and a superior room? Or had he brought her to his estate and ensconced her in guest quarters with which she was not acquainted? No matter. Henry had made certain she would be comfortable.

Uneasiness poured over her, replacing her feelings of love with fear. How could Henry have secured them a room at an inn or brought her to the estate? She recalled walking to meet Henry, but she had no memory of what had happened after that. Certainly she didn't recall a church, a ceremony, or a vicar pronouncing them man and wife.

Why not? Surely she had not partaken of stout ale so that her memory had been dulled or even eliminated. A gasp escaped her lips.

A sternly thin woman in the attire of a chambermaid entered. "Well, mercy me! Ye're finally awake, I see."

Disappointed to see a maid rather than her beloved, Abigail snapped, "So it would appear."

The woman's grim chuckle filled the room. "I see ye're not in much of a humor first thing in the mornin'. Are ye always like this?"

Always like this? Who would enjoy being greeted first

thing in the morning, in a strange bed, in an unknown room, in an undisclosed location, by a total stranger?

Forgetting her distress and puzzlement, Abigail recalled her own station. "You are the impudent one, whoever you are. If you continue in your disrespect, I shall inform the housekeeper."

As though the maid sought to spite Abigail, she flounced to one of the windows and drew back the drapes. Sunlight poured into the room.

Abigail squinted. "Close those curtains immediately! Do you not realize I have yet to get dressed?"

"Dressed? Ye shan't be gettin' dressed, M'lady. Ye'll be in bed for some time yet."

"In bed? You shall not tell me what to do!" Abigail leaped out of the high bed, forgetting that her feet would object to making contact with a cold floor. As her toes touched the wood, Abigail realized her extremities were the least of her problems. A wave of dizziness unexpectedly attacked. Too late, she clutched the covers. Instead of lending the support she needed to keep standing, they flew off the bed with her as she descended to the floor.

The maid ran to her side. "Don't ye be doin' such a foolish thing no more!" She took Abigail by the arm and helped her back into bed. Abigail realized she was too weak to object.

"What is the matter with me?"

"Ye're sick, that's what's the matter with ye."

"Sick?"

"What do ye expect, goin' out by yerself all times of night, with hardly enough fabric over ye to keep out a summer shower, much less the cold of a winter's eve?" Although with her dewy eyes and brilliant brown hair, the maid appeared younger than Abigail, she clucked like a mother hen. "And now here ye is, makin' more work fer me." The maid patted the edge of the covers firmly as if to emphasize her distress.

Abigail summoned up her remaining strength to issue an order that sounded adequately threatening. "You shall not speak that way to me. Whether I am causing you more work or not, you shall not reprimand me."

"I do remember my station and well at that, M'lady. I may be in charge of ye, but I work fer me own master."

"I beg your pardon. You must understand that I have no idea where I am. That fact, along with the great desire for a hot breakfast, is causing me to be in a foul temper."

"All is forgiven, M'lady."

"Thank you." Abigail knew she had been unsuccessful in keeping all traces of sarcasm from her voice. Seeking answers, she softened her tone. "Your own master? Do you mean Lord Hanover?" Abigail's heart began the beating so familiar when Henry's name fell from her lips.

"Lord Hanover?" The girl shook her head as though the very name were peculiar. She tucked Abigail back into bed, pulling the covers over her shoulders. "This Lord Hanover ye're speakin' of ain't my master."

"Then who is your master?"

She shrugged. "Ye need not vex yerself about such things. We'll take good care of ye."

Abigail sat back up, allowing the covers to fall to her waist. "I shall know now!" No sooner were the words out of her mouth than she felt a sudden urge to cough. Unable to control herself, she flew into a fit of hacking.

"Now, now, lie down there. I'll fluff the pillow so's ye can rest a bit upright, so that cold doesn't settle farther into yer chest." As the maid pulled the covers back over Abigail, she seemed sympathetic for the first time that morning. "I'm sure I can find ye another pillow so's you can have two. Wouldn't hurt ye none, in such a state ye are."

"Thank you."

"Ye're welcome." She placed her hands on her angular hips. "I don't mind ye none. I know ye're vexed. Delirious with fever, too, no doubt. Now ye just wait, and I'll be bringin' up some hot broth to make ye feel better soon." She tilted her head toward a bell setting on the table by the bed. "Ye might need to know, I'm Missy. Ye can ring that when ye need me.

Will there be anythin' else now?"

"Yes. You can tell me where I am. And where is Henry?"

"I don't know who Henry is, M'lady. Now just lie back and rest."

"I understand. Perhaps you only know him as Lord Hanover."

"No, M'lady."

Abigail fought the urge to cough. "In that case, I demand to see my father." To Abigail's dismay, she realized her voice showed all too well that she was too weak to make demands of anyone.

Missy shook her head, though the slow motion indicated more sympathy than malevolence. "I can't help ye."

How could that be? Surely Father wouldn't let her stay in a strange place. "I must send my father a message. Fetch me ink and paper."

"Ye are in no condition to write. Things will be settled. All in good time."

"All in good time? When is that, pray tell?" Abigail swallowed, resisting the tickle in her throat that pleaded with her to cough. "Does Father know where I am? Because I assure you, when he discovers you are keeping me a prisoner here, he shall take immediate action to see that you and your master, whoever he is, will suffer the most dire consequences."

"I think I'd best be gettin' the housekeeper." Missy curtsied and exited before Abigail could answer.

Abigail waited, eager to see the housekeeper. Surely she would provide answers.

Moments later, footfalls echoed in the hallway. Abigail put on her most authoritative face.

A thin woman entered. Her most distinguishing feature was her white-streaked black hair. The combination reminded Abigail of a skunk she'd seen in an illustrated book about animals of the Americas. Missy followed closely behind.

"Miss Pettigrew, I am Mrs. Farnsworth, the housekeeper." The thin woman's voice was as hard as Abigail imagined it would be.

"Yes." Despite her resolve to look self-assured, Abigail flinched.

"I understand you are having difficulty adjusting to your new situation."

"No difficulty. I merely asked your maid for answers."

"You are in no condition to make demands. You are here to get well. You will be told all you will need to know as soon as it is appropriate. In the meantime, cease asking our maid. She knows nothing."

"Then why will you not tell me?"

"All will be revealed in good time." The housekeeper looked down her nose at Abigail. "If you persist in vexing Missy, who is only following her orders, I shall have to tend to you myself." The housekeeper's scowl indicated she would find no pleasure in the task.

"Very well. But you will have your master to answer to once I am recovered."

"Yes, M'lady." Mrs. Farnsworth's voice held no warmth, fear, or apology. "Now then, will you be returning to your slumber, or shall I have Missy bring up a cup of broth?"

"Broth? Why, I was hoping for a nice bowl of hot oats and warm milk."

"Not with your sickness. You shall feast on broth or nothing."

Abigail opened her mouth to argue, but Mrs. Farnsworth had crossed her arms and planted both feet firmly on the polished floor.

"Very well," Abigail said with no enthusiasm. "I shall have the broth."

Mrs. Farnsworth gave her a nod of grudging approval. "Missy, please see to it that our guest gets her broth as soon as Cook prepares it."

"Yes, Mrs. Farnsworth." Missy looked at Abigail and broke out into a smile for the first time since she'd seen her. "That'll do ye good. Just ye rest now. I'll bring it up along shortly."

Too feeble to object, Abigail obeyed. Where was she? As she surrendered to unwanted sleep, she resolved to find out.

five

Days of warm broth and Missy's constant care soothed Abigail physically, but her soul was still grieved. Why hadn't Father visited? Surely she couldn't be so far away from home that he was unable to be with her. Could he be so angry that he didn't want to see her anymore? Had he disowned her?

Her fear-ridden thoughts turned defiant. What if he had? What did such a thing matter to her? If Father had disowned her, then she could still rely on her Henry.

The thought gave her untold consolation. Surely Henry would be arriving soon to save her. As soon as he discovered that Abigail was being held prisoner in a house unknown to her, he would be indignant, even furious. She imagined the enraged expression on his comely face. Realizing the situation was urgent, he would rush in and take her away.

Once he arrived at the estate, Henry was certain to locate her captor and unleash all his venom upon him. What sort of beast would delight in keeping a lady prisoner? The motive couldn't be blackmail. Abigail had no secrets to expose. In any event, surely a man who occupied such a stately residence had plenty of money at his disposal.

Abigail tried to picture the evil man who had brought her here, a monster who had swept her up after she had fainted so she would be unable to protest.

Perhaps he wore the finest fashions. But even the most finely sewn suit could not conceal his evil nature. No, he was sure to be hunchbacked, his ugly face dominated by a long, hooked nose and a few wisps of gray hair peeking from underneath his top hat. Dim eyes peered through slit lids. His skin was pockmarked. An open mouth revealed teeth of a most unpleasant yellowish brown. Abigail imagined the smell of cheap tobacco and sour wine hanging about him. Snuff stains dotted his neck cloth. She shuddered.

As soon as he laid eyes on this vile creature, Henry would be even more eager to rescue her. Maybe he would go so far as to challenge her captor to a duel!

If he did, she would be there to encourage him, to blow him a kiss or two in support of his bravery as he took his ten paces, weapon of choice in hand. A chill went through her as she pictured a silver dueling pistol with an ivory handle. But what if the kidnapper was a sharpshooter? Would Henry succumb. . . ?

No! The thought was too horrible.

Henry would be sure to win while defending her honor. Abigail looked about the lavish bedchamber. She recalled the many times over the past few days that Missy had served her, bringing her broth and making sure the fire was always lit. Abigail decided she didn't really want her captor to pay with his life. After all, he had kept her safe and made sure she was taken care of as she recovered from her illness.

Henry was a skilled enough marksman to shoot his pistol so that the bullet would merely graze the tip of her captor's hat. That was the best solution. Henry should teach him a lesson, that's all. Whoever her mysterious captor was, he had to learn that no gentleman goes about in the dark of night swooping up a lady as she waits to meet her beloved.

Abigail made a resolution. She would demand to speak to Henry before the duel, to make sure that the unknown man's hat would take the brunt of Henry's anger. She would have to plead with Henry to be merciful, of course, but she would be able to charm him into controlling his outrage. A wounded hat should be more than enough to frighten the beastly man into realizing that he should have never kept Abigail from her Henry!

Of course, Father would be present to witness the duel. How impressed he would be with Henry's marksmanship and courage! Surely such a display of true love and devotion would win Father's approval. Then nothing could stop them from marrying as planned, and all would be well.

Abigail sighed. Why did doubt continue to clutch her stomach with its icy fingers? She continued to feel a prompting to pray. Abigail closed her eyes, letting the prayer fall from her lips.

"Father in heaven," she murmured, "please let Henry find me soon. Please let him come and take me away from here." She paused before the next words escaped, almost against her will. "Lord, I know I should not have been a rebellious child. I should have obeyed Father, no matter what his motives for marrying me to someone I can never love. I know You hate rebellion, Lord. I know in my heart I deserve whatever punishment Thou meteth out to me. But Lord, I pray Thou wilt forgive me. And that Father will too."

The creaking of the door interrupted her prayer. Abigail opened her eyes.

"Well, that's good fer ye," Missy observed. "Repentance is always good for the soul."

"You heard me?" Embarrassed, Abigail averted her gaze. "I did not know you had entered."

"That's all right. I shan't tell anyone about yer private prayers to God." She sent Abigail a smile. "If anything, I'm mighty proud of ye. I misjudged ye, girl. The first day I met ye, I never thought I'd see ye so humble."

Abigail felt her cheeks flush hot at the reference to her rudeness toward the chambermaid, who had only been doing her job. She was eager to change the subject. "Has Father made any attempt to contact me?"

"I'm afraid not." Missy's forlorn look convinced Abigail that the maid felt sorry for her.

"Does he not know where I am staying?"

"Yea, I believe he does."

"Then why does he not send me a letter?" An uncertain feeling Abigail didn't like clutched at her stomach. "I wish he would say something. Anything. I would prefer to be chastened a million times over than to have him say nothing.

Unless," Abigail added, her voice brightening with hope, "he is too far away to make the journey."

Missy's gray eyes took on a sympathetic light. "Ye mean ye still don't know where ye are?"

"No." Even though Abigail felt well enough to emerge from bed and look out the window, she didn't recognize the grounds of the house she occupied.

Missy swallowed. "I ain't supposed to tell ye, but I just hate seein' a pretty girl so vexed. Ye're gettin' stronger ever' day. Ye'll be findin' out soon enough leastways." She paused.

Afraid that Missy might change her mind, Abigail prodded her. "Tell me, Missy. Where am I?"

"I'd rather not, if I can help it." She brightened. "Do ye feel like risin' out of the bed?"

Abigail nodded.

"Then why don't ye look out the window again?"

Obeying, Abigail threw the covers back and slid out of bed. When her feet touched the cold floor, she didn't mind. Just having permission to stand upright was reason enough for celebration. She stood in place for a moment to get her bearings.

"Are ye all right?" Missy inquired.

"Yes." She took a few steps to the window and stared out. Dormant gardens and bare trees greeted her. "Perhaps I would recognize the front lawn."

"Ye are lookin' at the front lawn," Missy informed her. "Don't ye recognize the grounds?"

"I'm afraid not."

Abigail heard the maid let out a tired sigh. "I shouldn't be surprised. The old master was a recluse for so long that nary a celebration has taken place here in years. I remember well the parties and balls that went on when the lady of the house was alive."

Curious, Abigail turned to face Missy. "The lady of the house?"

Missy looked at Abigail, but the glassy appearance of her

eyes told her the maid was somewhere else in spirit, perhaps at an extravagant ball that had taken place many years in the past. She shook her head. "I thought the place might wake up again when the young masters finished their educations, but. . ." The maid sighed. "Oh, never mind. It's a sin to pine away for somethin' that can never be. As for you, I'm supposin' there's no other way. I'll tell ye. But first ye must get back in bed."

Abigail quickly obeyed.

As Missy drew the covers over her young charge, she added, "And ye have to promise not to let on ye found out from me."

"I promise."

"You're at the Sutton estate."

"Pray tell!" Abigail gasped. "The Sutton estate?" She took a moment to let the information sink in. Her head shook in violent denial. "No! How can that be?"

"Ye don't remember?"

"No." Abigail had tried so many times to recall the events of the night that Henry and she were supposed to marry. She remembered walking to the churchyard to meet him, shivering in a velvet cape hardly sufficient for fighting off the cold. The night had been gloomy, with a freezing drizzle. The memory made her tremble even now.

Had she gone through this ordeal just to face more humiliation? The embarrassment that not only had her beloved Henry been late for their meeting, but that he had never shown up at all? That he had allowed the hateful rogue, Lord Sutton, to take her?

"No, I do not remember," Abigail repeated.

"I do," Missy said. "Ye were quite chilled. What were ye doin' out there in the freezing night, all alone, with barely a decent wrap?"

"That is none of your affair," she snapped.

"Is that so, now?" Missy shrugged. "I suppose ye're right."

Anger replaced chagrin. "Did he tell you why he brought me here?"

Missy let out a grim chuckle. "I'm supposin' he didn't want to leave ye out there to catch yer death."

"So he just happened to be passing by at that moment? None of this was planned?"

"As far as I know." Missy cast her a look of bewilderment. "What makes ye think he'd be out in the middle of the night lookin' fer lasses to pick up, eh?"

"Nothing," Abigail admitted to Missy. Under her breath, she added, "Although I would not be surprised to learn if he didn't wander the streets looking for amusement."

"What was that? You think me master wanders the streets?"

"My observation was not for your ears."

"Then don't talk loud enough for a body to hear." Missy tilted her head. "What makes ye think m'lord is so unsavory?"

Abigail was tempted to tell Missy all about her master's reputation as a cad, but she thought better of it. "If you do not know already, then I shall not tell you."

"That's fer the best. Lord Sutton has always been nothin' but kind to me. I shall defend him 'til the day I die."

"Is that so? To each his own, then." Abigail wondered how anyone could be so loyal to a man with such an undesirable reputation. "I suppose his behavior matters not to you, as long as your wages are paid."

"And fer that ye should be thankful," Missy pointed out. "Seein' as ye're not the one payin' wages fer me to be here with ye every day. Now if there'll be nothin' else, I'll be bringin' yer meal to ye at the stroke of six."

"That will be all."

Missy curtsied and exited, leaving Abigail to fume. After pondering her situation, she realized why Father had not visited. "He wants me to stay here and recover, just so I shall feel obliged to Lord Sutton. Then I shall have to marry him!" The thought caused so much rage to stir within her that Abigail once again was attacked by another episode of coughing.

As she hacked her way through the fit, Missy returned, rushing to her bedside. "Are ye all right?" As though the motion would help her to speak, Missy administered several hard whacks on her back. Not wishing to suffer more, Abigail forced herself to stop coughing.

"I am quite well now," she assured the maid.

Missy gave her a knowing nod as she handed Abigail a glass of tepid water. "I thought so. Nothin' like a few good pats on the back to bring up the stuff ye're tryin' to get rid of."

Abigail grimaced. "I suppose such a state of sickness hardly makes me appear the lady."

"Sickness don't do much for nobody. 'Cept maybe bring out their true character."

Abigail wondered what the maid meant. She decided not to ask.

"Oh my, I almost forgot." Missy reached her hand in the pocket of her dress. "I have a letter fer ye."

"A letter?" Abigail's gasp threw her into another fit of coughing.

Missy hurried over to pat Abigail's back. "If ye get this excited, I won't be gettin' yer mail to ye."

"Oh, no," she protested between coughs. "Please do not keep me from my letters."

"All right. I know ye must be lonely, with no one but me to talk to."

Abigail swallowed. Missy was right, but Abigail didn't have the heart to admit it. She knew the girl was trying her best in her own way to make Abigail comfortable and to provide as much in the way of companionship as she could. Thankfully, Missy didn't wait for Abigail to answer before handing her the letter.

She recognized the fine ivory-colored paper and the seal of the Pettigrew family crest. Large letters scrawled in black ink were as familiar to her as her own handwriting. A victorious smile tickled her lips. Father was writing to announce his imminent arrival to rescue her!

She could not will her heart to stop its rapid beating, nor could she stop her hands from shaking so badly that Missy was sure to notice. Embarrassed, she swallowed, which led to a renewed series of coughs.

"Goodness, Child," Missy consoled, whacking her back. "Don't be gettin' yerself so excited now."

Abigail nodded, though she had no idea how to obey Missy's wise counsel. How could she be expected to control the emotions set free by the thought of liberty?

After Abigail's coughing subsided, Missy asked permission to leave. Abigail happily granted it. As soon as the maid disappeared, Abigail tore open the letter and scanned its contents:

Dear Abigail,

As you have likely surmised, I have been informed of your wild adventure, wandering about unescorted in the night. No doubt you realize that I cannot express the extent of my surprise, horror, and disappointment in you. Never in my wildest imaginations did I fathom you would ever undertake such unbecoming behavior, behavior most inappropriate to a lady of the Pettigrew household.

I pray you are thanking Providence that you were rescued by your host. As you have most likely learned by now, he did indeed bring you, half-conscious, to our estate in the middle of the night. Your stepmother was awake, having realized your absence when she checked your bed. Considerate of my feelings as always, she had not informed me of your deceit. Only later did she relate to me the anxiety she experienced worrying about you throughout the night, pacing the kitchen alone as I slept, blissfully unaware of my own daughter's treachery.

Hours passed before your host rode up to our door, your limp figure barely clinging to the horse. What a fright you caused your dear stepmother, who has nothing but your best interests at heart, as she imagined you were dead! When she learned the truth—that you had not expired but had merely fainted—her fright turned to consternation and great anxiety over how learning about your behavior would vex me. Unlike you, Abigail, she wanted to consider my feelings. Therefore, she chose not to awaken me. When your host gallantly offered to take you to his estate, she accepted, knowing this event would assure I would remain asleep and be spared the humiliation of discovering your treachery in such a shocking manner. Her plan was to tell me herself the next morning, then send for you right away.

Your stepmother did not realize at the time that you had foolishly chosen not to wear a proper winter coat, which, as you now know, resulted in your illness. When we learned this, all parties involved thought it best to allow you to remain where you currently reside, lest increased exposure to the cold outside air cause your illness to lead to your untimely demise.

I trust now that time has passed, you are feeling better. My wish and desire is for you to return to your full state of youthful health. I pray that is God's desire as well.

I hope you will take full advantage of this distress to meditate upon the unhappiness you have caused both of us and on the disgrace you have brought upon the Pettigrew name, and that after you are well in body, you will return to us a repentant soul.

In the meanwhile, I shall take your stepmother's suggestion that I not make further contact with you until such time arrives. While I regret that I will not be able to see you, I believe her counsel is wise.

Yours,
Father

Abigail's hand shook as she read and reread the letter. Obviously, Father had no plans to take her away from this place in the foreseeable future. She reread the last part of the message. How could he not see her, not even write? How much time would he allow to pass? Certainly Griselda would like the time to be indefinite. Abigail knew her father was punishing her. Perhaps he was only too happy that his wife had suggested such harsh treatment of his wayward daughter.

And to think that he left her there, despite the potential scandal. Would the whole world talk about the little Pettigrew girl, locked up in a strange estate away from her home and family? Apparently, her father no longer cared about her or her reputation.

"Oh, Father!" she cried to the man who could not hear her. "Have I hurt you so much?"

Abigail knew the answer. She had risked throwing away everything she held dear when she had tried to elope with Henry. The risk had failed. If she cared not a bit about her own reputation, why should they? The reality of her actions and her present situation weighed upon her.

She wondered how long he thought she should remain away from her own home and family. Until she was well? How long would that be?

"How can I bear it?"

A torrent of tears flowed before she could contain them. She sought a kerchief from the nightstand drawer. Grateful to discover one, she used it to wipe her eyes. She sniffled.

Missy's footsteps in the hall alerted her to the fact she would soon have companionship. The maid would likely be full of questions about the letter's contents. Abigail was in no humor to share them. She slipped the piece of paper in the folds of her nightshift and dove under the covers. She did not want Missy to see her reddened and wet face, and maybe if she pretended to be asleep, the girl would go away.

Her wishes were not to be granted. A shock of frigid air hit her as Missy threw back the coverlet. "Time to rise, M'lady."

"Time to rise?" In her surprise, Abigail forgot that she didn't want Missy to see her tear-streaked face. "I thought you wanted me to stay in bed."

"I did. But that was before." Missy scrutinized Abigail. "Ye are still coughin', but seein' as you could stand without help today, methinks ye're well enough. As long as ye're careful to wear enough clothin', that is."

"Well enough? Well enough for what?"

"The master," Missy said matter-of-factly, as though Abigail shouldn't harbor the least bit of surprise. "He is home. It is time for ye to meet him."

six

"Meet him? But I have no desire to meet anyone who would keep me captive in his house against my will!" Abigail crossed her arms over her chest. With all her strength, she anchored herself on the bed. If Missy wanted her to move, she would have to take her by force.

"Against yer will, eh?" Missy placed her hands on her hips. "Fine then." She nodded once and swept her hand toward the door of the bedchamber. "Ye can go right ahead and leave."

Abigail's heart seemed to leap out of her throat with joy. "I can?"

"Sure ye can." Missy's mouth tightened. "Ye could have left any time ye liked."

"Is that so? Why did you not tell me before?"

Abigail soared out of bed, ready to take Missy at her word. She was so thrilled by the prospect of escape that she barely noticed the wooziness she was accustomed to feeling upon standing was now gone. She swirled in delight.

"Feelin' better, I see," Missy commented.

"Yes—" The wooziness suddenly returned. Abigail stopped in midturn and placed a hand to her forehead.

Missy hastened to her side. She placed a comforting arm around Abigail's waist to steady her. "Are ye sure ye're well enough to rise out of bed?"

"Perhaps not as well as I first thought." She released herself from Missy's hold and crawled back up into the bed. She remained sitting upright, letting her legs dangle off the side of the high mattress. "You said I could leave at any time. I beg to differ. How could I have left when I could not stand upright?"

Missy sniffed. "I suppose me master should have left ye out there in the cold." She shrugged. "Perhaps Vicar Morrison would have happened along eventually. Maybe in time to save yer life, maybe not." The look Missy sent Abigail was cold, as though she cared not a whit whether Abigail lived or died.

Hurt feelings tugged at Abigail, indicating she had become fonder of Missy's company than she had intended. "That would not be your wish, would it? For me to die?"

"Of course not, silly goose." Missy shook her head. "But I hate to see ye so ungrateful."

Remorse washed over Abigail. "I suppose your master meant well." She sent Missy a meaningful look. "But once I speak to him, I shall be on my way."

"Very well." Missy's tone was chilly. "I'll be leavin' ye to get dressed, unless ye'd like me to help." Missy's expression was apologetic. "I'm afraid we don't have a proper ladies' maid."

"Of course not." Why would the Suttons employ a ladies' maid? No female had lived at the estate since Lady Elizabeth's death.

Abigail remembered the frock she had been wearing that fateful night when she was to meet her beloved Henry. She had dressed without assistance. Abigail hadn't dared summon the Pettigrew maid to help with her garment. Assuming Hilda would agree to assist her, she would have most certainly betrayed Abigail's elopement plans to Griselda immediately upon learning them.

Soon after Father's wedding, Abigail's own maid had been dismissed in favor of keeping Griselda's. Griselda always enjoyed Hilda's services first, while Abigail was left with whatever time Hilda could spare. The dismissal of Abigail's maid had occurred ostensibly from a desire to economize, but Abigail suspected Griselda's ulterior motive was to keep as many servants with allegiance to her in the Pettigrew household as possible. Whatever old servants she couldn't order the housekeeper to fire outright, Griselda had done her best to alienate until only Mattie and Father's valet remained. Griselda had hired everyone else.

Abigail sighed.

"I know," Missy answered.

Abigail lurched back to the present. "What?"

"Yer dress, of course."

Missy held Abigail's dress up for inspection. The emerald green silk had become wrinkled and matted to such an extent that Abigail failed to see how it could be smoothed back into place. She gasped.

"It's a cryin' shame," Missy agreed. "It sure don't look like much now, but I venture it was mighty pretty before it got all wet."

"Obviously, no one took the time or effort to press it." Abigail tried to rein in her anger at the ruin of her favorite dress.

"I suppose not, M'lady." Missy grimaced, her face turning an unflattering shade of red. "I most humbly beg your pardon."

The maid's apology gave Abigail pause. She tried to consider the situation from Missy's point of view. "That is quite all right. In all the confusion and without a proper ladies' maid, I venture your last thought was that the dress needed proper care."

"Yes, M'lady."

Abigail wished she hadn't left her leather satchel on her bed the night of the failed elopement. Had she not been wild with excitement at the prospect of a secret marriage, she would have had the presence of mind to take it and would at this moment have a second dress to wear. Mulling over her options, she wondered if she could send a messenger to the Pettigrew estate to secure her one or two more dresses.

No. The time had passed for such plans. For a brief moment, she considered asking if any of Lady Elizabeth's garments remained in her closet. Just as quickly she bit back the question. She had no right to don a dead lady's clothing, and Lord Sutton would hardly find her appealing in his mother's dress.

"M'lady, do ye want me to stay?"

Abigail nodded. "I suppose I could use some help." She shot Missy a pleading look. "Perchance do you have any skill in dressing hair?"

Missy's dark eyebrows arched. "Ye wish me to dress yer hair? Whatever for?"

"A lady must look her best at all times. Do you not agree?"

Abigail concealed her real motive. She wanted to appear as beautiful as possible when she confronted the master of the estate. Let him see that she, Abigail Pettigrew, was a lady of quality. Let him be grieved to see her depart.

"I suppose I could try." Missy moved toward her and examined Abigail's honey blond locks with a discerning eye. She lifted a few strands and swished them back and forth between her fingers. "Yer hair's gotten a mite straggly. I'm afraid makin' it pretty won't be easy."

"I beg your pardon!"

Missy backed away and curtsied. "Forgive me, M'lady. I'm not used to doin' much but tryin' to keep me own hair from fallin' in me face while I scrub the floors." Missy studied her charge. "I doubt I can do ye justice."

Imitating Missy's earlier gesture, Abigail twisted a few strands of poker straight hair between her own thumb and forefinger. Missy was right. Her crowning glory was all the worse for not having been groomed during her illness.

"That is quite all right. I know you will do your best." Abigail hoped the smile she plastered on her face didn't reveal her discouragement and doubt.

Missy sent Abigail a relieved grin before she tilted her head toward the oak vanity chair. "Why don't I help ye with yer dress? Then I'll see what I can do."

❧

Tedric waited for Abigail in the study. He leaned back in the well-worn brown mahogany chair. The chair, along with the carved desk, had been in his family since Grandfather Sutton's day. Shelves of books lined the wall behind Tedric. He took comfort in their presence. Each volume had a special place on its shelf. Tedric had read almost all of them, whether the language was English, Latin, Greek, or French.

For the first time in his life, Tedric almost wished he couldn't read. In his hand, he held a letter from Henry Hanover, bearing the Hanover family crest on creamy paper. Tedric reread the tiny scrawl. Not only had Henry left Abigail standing in a freezing rain with little to shield her but hopes of becoming his wife, but also he had no intention of honoring his promise to marry her. Not now. Not ever.

Adding insult to injury, Henry had written a letter to convey the news. The fact that Henry knew Tedric would be required to pay postage to receive the letter was of little importance except that it revealed Henry was cheap as well as inconsiderate. A gentleman would have been courteous enough to visit Abigail in person.

Tedric let out a harrumph. He had never heard the name "Henry Hanover" and the word "gentleman" spoken in the same breath. So why should Henry's behavior surprise him?

Even so, Tedric didn't understand how Henry could be so cruel. Tedric had never been friends with Henry, even though they were close in age and attended many of the same social gatherings. Intimate knowledge of Tedric's own brother, Cecil, was enough to fill his gullet with the skillful deceptions of the garden-variety rake. Tedric guessed that Henry expected Cecil would be the one to convey his message to Abigail. Surely Cecil had experience enough in breaking women's hearts.

If only Cecil hadn't been detained in London. Tedric grimaced. Cecil had pleaded for more time to deal with London's chronically clogged courts. Tedric suspected that the city's gambling establishments as well as gatherings in houses of both respectable and ill repute were of far more interest to his brother than the rather dull details of the estate's business.

Tedric grimaced. He dreaded the moment Abigail would walk through the polished wood doorway to the study. How could he tell her that Henry had abandoned her forever? Not that Tedric faulted Abigail for wanting to escape marriage to Cecil. Tedric understood that Cecil didn't love her. Certainly Abigail was painfully aware of the fact herself. Perhaps that's why she had attempted the ill-fated elopement.

Still, for Cecil's sake and for the Sutton family honor, Tedric knew he would have to be strict with his prospective sister-in-law. He would be forced to act as a father, explaining that her betrothal to a Sutton meant that proper behavior was expected.

Most women of her station would be contrite, admitting their mistake, perhaps summoning a few tears for good measure. Tedric wasn't so sure about Abigail. He hadn't seen her since the night he'd found her listless body in the churchyard. He hadn't meant to frighten her so. Guilt about how he must have scared the poor thing out of her wits haunted him. But what if he hadn't happened by? Or worse, what if he had been like the priest in the Bible story of the Good Samaritan, leaving Abigail to fend for herself? Many gentlemen might have chosen that course rather than to risk humiliating the daughter of an esteemed family. Abigail surely had suffered untold embarrassment. But since he'd happened by to rescue her from the freezing drizzle, at least she hadn't had to pay for her mistake with her life.

Tedric wondered what had possessed Abigail to associate with a cad such as Henry. He twitched his mouth into a knowing line. Henry was handsome, for certain. Rogues always were. No doubt Henry was smooth enough to flatter a young woman unwise to the ways of the world, easily luring her into his web of lies.

He thought about his fiery little Abigail. How was she to know that someone like Henry would never marry a woman whose family was nearly impoverished? Surely Abigail had been reared with the confidence of her unblemished family name. Certainly she could see that her family didn't live as well as some of the other nearby aristocracy. Yet she lacked for nothing. How could she be expected to know the realities of how much money was needed to keep an estate running?

He knew one fact. If God ever chose to bless him with a daughter, or many daughters, Tedric would make certain they would have nothing to bother their pretty little heads except choosing what dress to wear to the next party.

In a flash, his imagination conjured up a young girl, the portrait of what his daughter with Abigail might look like. She was a petite, dark-haired beauty, with his blue eyes and Abigail's lithe frame and flawless skin.

"Stop it!" Tedric jumped in his seat. To his shock, he had uttered the words aloud.

"Thou shalt not covet thy neighbour's house, thou shalt not covet thy neighbour's wife, nor his manservant, nor his maid-servant, nor his ox, nor his ass, nor any thing that is thy neighbour's." The admonition of Exodus 20:17 rolled through his brain. Repentant, Tedric petitioned silently for the Lord's forgiveness.

What kind of brother was he, to be thinking of Cecil's betrothed in such a manner? And what kind of brother-in-law would he be to Abigail if he didn't put such nonsense out of his mind here and now?

At that moment, the butler entered. "Miss Abigail Pettigrew is here to see you."

Tedric's stomach lurched with anticipation and dread. Nevertheless, he managed a curt nod. "Send her in."

seven

Abigail walked woozily down a wide hall, following the butler. Her footfalls remained silent upon the well-worn but still beautiful Oriental runner. Occasionally, she lifted her gaze to walls painted a muddy green. Portraits in gilded frames, presumably of long-dead lords and ladies, were spaced apart in exact measurement. The eyes of each ancestor stared at her as though the subjects of the pictures had come alive for the sheer purpose of scrutinizing her. Superior stares they were indeed.

One full-length painting showed a young man in a powdered wig with the large, stiff collar dictated by past fashion. The man held a falcon, a hunting bird favored by the wealthy. The portrait beside his appeared to have been painted about the same time. The powder-haired woman was wearing enough brocade, lace, and rubies so that one could almost overlook her hooked nose.

Abigail sniffled as though to remind herself that her nose was far from hooked. Its diminutive size caused it to be barely noticeable. With a proud motion, she corrected her posture. Then, recalling a flaw in her appearance, she touched a loose curl. Abigail tried not to feel self-conscious about the inept way in which Missy had dressed her hair. Perhaps if she pretended that Hilda had styled her honey blond locks, her confidence would overwhelm Lord Sutton so he wouldn't notice that her coiffure was lopsided.

She tried not to look down at her crumpled skirt. Optimistic, she decided to be grateful that the dampness hadn't shrunk her dress beyond her ability to squeeze her frame into the garment. Then again, she wasn't quite as filled out as she had been on the day of her failed elopement. Warm broth did little to stick to one's ribs.

She tugged on the lace of her left sleeve. Miraculously, the fragile decoration had borne no damage. No seams had broken. The dress even retained all its buttons. She surmised she could look much worse.

Perhaps if she stared straight ahead, Lord Sutton would concentrate on her face and be blind to the fact that her dress had suffered from its prolonged exposure to freezing drizzle.

She held her shoulders back and straightened herself to her full height. Abigail strove not to look arrogant. Her aim was simply to exude confidence—more confidence than she felt. She had long awaited the moment when she could confront her captor. Now that the time had finally arrived, why was her self-assurance waning?

The uniformed butler paused in front of a door at the end of the hall. He turned toward her and nodded. For an instant, Abigail froze in place. She wondered if she could pretend to faint so she wouldn't have to face such a beast. Her knees began to feel so wobbly that she wondered if she might faint for real. Abigail told herself she was still feeling the effects of her illness and shaky knees were to be expected.

After the butler announced her, Abigail listened for a response. Apparently, Lord Sutton merely nodded, giving the butler permission to look her way.

"You may enter," he prodded, his expressionless face not revealing what he thought of his temporary charge.

Abigail nodded and forced herself to walk past the butler and over the threshold. Her initial impression of the room was that of a large, dark cave, not unlike her father's study at home—down to the same centuries-old furniture carved so heavily that not an inch seemed to be untouched by a knife. She observed a figure standing behind a large desk but framed by an expansive collection of books. She took in a deep breath and lifted her face. She stared straight into startling blue eyes. Abigail gasped.

"It is you!" Her shriek defied all good intentions to appear poised.

His eyes widened in obvious shock at her outburst, but otherwise he remained calm. "I do not believe we have been properly introduced. I beg your forgiveness at the informality necessitated by our current circumstances. I am Tedric Sutton. I am honored that you have been a guest in my home during your illness, and I pray that you have been treated well."

Lord Sutton.

Remembering her manners, she curtsied reflexively, despite the fact that such a vile man deserved no respect.

She looked back up onto his countenance. So this was the man Father wanted her to marry! The man who stopped to speak to her the night she was writing in her diary. The man who charged her with the phrase "peppery." Indeed!

She opened her mouth to admonish him; but his searching eyes, filled with wonder and kindness, stopped her.

Her anger evaporated. Rather than feeling threatened, a sense of safety and security took hold of her. Somehow, she knew that as long as she trusted this man, he would protect her. Yet Lord Sutton was a known rake and gambler. Perhaps this was his stock in trade, to deceive innocent women. Flashing blue eyes, a straight nose, and wavy ebony hair would be enough to draw the attention of any woman, enough to lure an innocent into thinking he loved her, only to leave her alone and abandoned, her heart broken.

Father in heaven, I pray you will help me not succumb to his lies!

Abigail felt a sense of peace. She observed the face of her host. Anyone could see that he was outwardly handsome. Honing in on his eyes, Abigail wondered about the state of his soul. When she studied his face, she could feel emanating from him a sense of peace, a peace she found only in those persons in whom the Lord dwelt. Instinctively, she felt that he belonged to the Lord Jesus Christ. But how could that be? Could the rumors whispered in local drawing rooms be wrong?

"The illness has temporarily claimed some of your faculties.

Quite understandable." His eyes reflected the compassion in his words.

Abigail felt her cheeks flush. Having merely uttered his name and dropped an awkward curtsey, of course she appeared to be a ninny. Abigail stood up to her full height. Rather than empowering her, she felt more helpless as she still craned her neck to meet his gaze. "I beg your pardon. My faculties are at their peak." She was pleased that her voice bespoke bravado.

"Then I most humbly beg your pardon. Please, take a seat." He nodded toward a stiff wooden chair.

"I shall stand, thank you. What I have to say will not take but a moment."

He arched a dark eyebrow. "I am most interested in what you have to say to me."

She drew a breath. "I–I. . ."

Why couldn't she say anything?

"Perhaps you plan to tell me that Henry Hanover will soon arrive to rescue you?" His voice held no rancor.

Abigail's stomach felt as though it were about to jump into her throat. "Henry? Who told you about him?"

"He did."

"He did?" Her stomach lurched with anticipation. "He has already been here to see you?" A triumphant smile touched her lips. "I am sure he was quite indignant that you took me away from the churchyard before he could arrive."

A shadow of a smile touched his lips. "On the contrary, some would say that I saved your life."

"Some would be quite mistaken." Abigail nodded once in confirmation. "Henry would have been along soon enough. Rather than saving my life, you interrupted our plans. Surely he was quite angry with you?"

Ignoring her question, Tedric took hold of a letter lying on his desk and waved it before her. Abigail recognized that the letter bore the Hanover family seal.

"He tried to contact me? He sent me a letter?" Abigail's

voice revealed the combination of happiness and outrage she felt. "You beast! How dare you keep my letter! Let me have that!" She extended her hand to grab it.

Tedric drew his hand back so that the letter missed her grasp. "But it is not addressed to you. It was sent to me."

Abigail's mouth dropped open as she let her hand drop to her side. How could Henry send a letter to Lord Sutton and not to her?

"I am sure he had discovered the nature of your illness and thought it best to communicate with me rather than you directly," Tedric explained, as though he could read Abigail's thoughts. Why didn't Tedric seem to believe what he was telling her?

Curiosity overruled humiliation. "What did he say?" As soon as the question left her lips, she became all too aware of her beating heart.

"Would you care to read it yourself?" He extended the hand that held the letter tantalizingly within her reach. His blue eyes seemed moist, almost as though his own heart were about to shatter.

Nodding, she took the envelope gently from his grasp. Recalling his offer that she be seated, Abigail followed her instincts and took her place in the unyielding chair before reading:

Dear Tedric,

I have come to understand that you are accommodating in your home a lady of my acquaintance, Abigail Pettigrew, as she recovers from a grave illness. Hence, I am sending you this correspondence rather than posting it directly to the Pettigrew estate. I have already sent a letter of apology by post to Abigail's father.

It has been brought to my attention that Miss Pettigrew misunderstood my kind attentions toward her as gestures of more than the fondest friendship and esteem. She is young, as you are aware, so it is quite understandable that she might misconstrue a gentleman's intentions. To my utmost shock and regret, she came to believe we were engaged. Without any encouragement, she decided to meet me the night you discovered her in the churchyard.

Abigail gasped. Misunderstood? How could she have misunderstood his promise that she would become his wife that very night? No. It couldn't be. She kept reading:

For your discovery and rescue of her, I am most grateful. However, I am quite distressed by the thought that she might still believe we are betrothed. We are not.

Not betrothed? Not betrothed? No!

In fact, I am engaged to marry a fine lady here in London. I believe you met her at Baron von Stein's ball last season—Lady Hempstead.

"Lady Hempstead?" Abigail cried. She shook her head in disbelief and looked at Tedric. "He is betrothed to a dowager?"

"Lady Ernestine Hempstead," Tedric answered. "The widow of the viscount of Hempstead."

"She must be quite old."

"At least thirty-five," Tedric told her.

"But why would he want to marry an old woman?" Abigail wondered aloud. *When he could have me!*

The corners of Tedric's mouth took a slight upward turn. "The early bloom of youth has passed her by, but the dowager has approached the season of a more mature beauty. She also has great land holdings and a considerable fortune."

The realization of Abigail's changed situation suddenly struck her with the force of a kick from a horse's hoof. "Then he is not coming," she whispered. "Henry is not going to take me away from here."

"No he is not, and I regret how that news must be of great disappointment to you."

Unable to answer, Abigail stared at her wrinkled skirt.

Tedric's voice took on the tone of a disciplinarian. "Your father has arranged for you to become Lady Sutton. My family can forgive you this youthful indiscretion. But as you wait for your wedding day and for the gossip to die, you are to take no more actions that will bring disgrace to the Sutton name." He paused. "I want you to forget you ever met Henry Hanover."

Her eyes met his once again. Abigail rose. "I beg your pardon! Forget I ever met Henry? Do you think you can order me to forget the man I love?"

"The man you love? Do not be preposterous. You are no sophisticated London society matron. How are you to know what love is?"

"I do know! More than you ever will!" Abigail stamped her foot.

Tedric folded his arms. "Obviously you do. Any lady who displays such maturity must be experienced in the ways of love."

"Why, you. . .you!" Unable to verbalize her rage, Abigail couldn't refrain from stamping her foot once more. Feeling the blood pump to her face, she knew she was turning a most unflattering shade of crimson. The grin on Tedric's face revealed his high amusement.

"Think of me what you like," she finally spit out, "but you can no longer keep me here against my will. I shall be leaving. Now." She crossed her arms and narrowed her eyes at him. "Summon your carriage."

"I would be happy to oblige," he answered. "It is my wish for my guests to enjoy, not to rue, my hospitality."

Abigail raised her eyebrows and crooked her mouth in victory. She had won! Not only would she be leaving the Sutton estate once and for all, but as soon as she returned to her own home, she would convince Father to call off the betrothal.

The wheels in her mind spun. First, she would charm her father. If that didn't work, she would beg. Plead. Promise him anything.

Abigail glanced in the direction of the handsome man standing before her. He wore well the chiseled features and fine white teeth of an aristocrat and cut a fine form in his expertly tailored suit. Yes, she would beg Father to break off the betrothal. She looked at the man standing before her again. Unless, perhaps, Tedric showed himself worthy of her affections.

"I am glad you see things my way," she said aloud.

The look of regret that flashed across his face almost was enough to make her wish she hadn't made her feelings known so blatantly.

Tedric's attention remained upon her for only a moment. The next instant, he looked beyond her. "There you are, Ralph. I was just about to ring for you. Would you instruct Nathan to ready the carriage? Miss Pettigrew will be returning to her estate tonight."

"Yes. But first, if I may deliver to you this letter. It just arrived by messenger from the Pettigrew estate."

"But of course." Tedric took the letter from the butler's hand and then read the name. "It is for you." He relinquished the envelope to Abigail.

"Father wrote!" she exclaimed, thinking her father might have reconsidered his decision not to contact her again for awhile. Her elation was short-lived. As soon as she saw her name written on the envelope, she knew. The script belonged not to Father, but to her stepmother.

"Griselda." Venom was apparent in her voice. "What could she possibly have to say to me?"

eight

"You hardly seem happy at the prospect of receiving a letter from your stepmother," Tedric noted. "Is there reason for you to be upset?"

Abigail noticed the concern evident in his face. Her fears softened, and her heart beat a little less rapidly. She sank into the chair. "I hope not. I mean to say, I am sure there is not." She opened the letter, praying that Tedric wouldn't notice that her hands shook.

Greetings, Abigail,

I trust this letter finds you well on your way to recovery. You are lucky to be so well cared for at the Sutton estate. Few girls in your situation would be as fortunate.

I hope you have had time to contemplate your actions and the pain they have brought to your father. He has not shared the depth of his feelings with anyone, but I know he is stricken with grief by your rebellion. You should be thoroughly ashamed of yourself.

Despite all this, I know that you no doubt nurse feelings that you should be returning here to resume your life with your father and me forthwith. Exhume those thoughts from your mind. For you see, I am with child.

A gasp escaped Abigail's lips. "With child!"

"With child? Who is with child?" Tedric asked.

Abigail tried not to grimace, lest Tedric think her jealous of a new little brother or sister. "My stepmother."

"Oh." He raised his eyebrows. "Are you suggesting this news comes as a complete shock?"

Abigail set her gaze upon the folds of her skirt. She knew

Griselda was young and that children were the natural result of a marital union. Yet somehow, she hadn't pictured that Father would wish for a new family. Wasn't she enough? She knew she hadn't been the perfect daughter or the flawless stepdaughter, but hadn't she been good enough?

"I beg your pardon," Tedric apologized, interrupting her musings. "I should not have spoken to a lady about such indelicate matters."

As if you would know, since the women of your acquaintance are hardly ladies. Abigail bit back her retort. "It is not that. . . ," she murmured. Having no idea what else to say, she clamped her mouth shut.

Tedric was not so reticent. " 'Wrath is cruel, and anger is outrageous; but who is able to stand before envy?' "

As soon as the meaning of the words registered, rage hit Abigail as though God Himself had pitched forked lightning straight through her heart. "Envy?" Abigail jumped to her feet. "How dare you quote Proverbs to me!"

How dare he, indeed? How did this man, who knew nothing about her, manage to see through her as though she were made of lace?

"I–I—" Abigail felt a surge of heat flow into her body, a sure sign she was about to lose control of her ire. "I shall be leaving this instant!"

She turned her back to him, determined to exit immediately even if she had to kick down the heavy mahogany door with her leather-clad feet.

"No, you shall not." His voice was sharp enough to stop her in midstep.

Without bothering to turn back to face him, she lifted her nose in the air and retorted, "Are you suggesting you can stop me?"

"It is not I who will try to stop you." The edge had left his tone.

"Oh?" Abigail twirled a half circle and faced him. Once again, she noticed the brilliant color of his eyes. Forcing her attraction aside, she reminded herself that Tedric was the enemy. "If you will not stop me, then who will?"

"Your family."

"And how shall that be? They are not here." Or were they? For a moment, her heart beat with hope. Was Father waiting for her in the parlor at this very moment?

"Unless Father has arrived." Her voice grew stronger with conviction. "And if he has, he shall have plenty to say to you."

"Perhaps he will when we do finally meet. But I am afraid that will have to wait." Tedric's regret seemed genuine. "It is not the desire of your father or stepmother that you should leave here."

"My stepmother holds no jurisdiction over my father."

"Aye, but he sent me a letter as well. He asked me if I would kindly allow you to remain here until the weather breaks in the spring."

"The spring? But spring is months away! There is no reason to keep me here. I am perfectly well."

Tedric shook his head. "You know as well as I do that Dr. Riley does not agree."

"That old coot? What does he know?" Abigail said with a sniff.

"He knows enough about medicine to keep you from putting other family members in jeopardy. Surely you have no desire to bring any sickness into your house, particularly with your stepmother in her delicate condition."

Guilt pricked Abigail. "No, I suppose not," she was forced to admit. An unsettling thought occurred to her. "But my clothes! What shall I do? I cannot wear Missy's nightshift and this wrinkled dress forever." She crinkled a bunch of the green silk skirt in her fist.

"Of course not. Your other clothes have already been sent. You will find that your trunk awaits you in your bedchamber."

"Oh." Father—or perhaps Griselda—had thought of everything. Defeated, Abigail took her seat and read the rest of Griselda's letter. Its contents only served to confirm what

Tedric said. Abigail would be staying at the Sutton estate. For a shining moment, she considered writing Father to implore him to change his mind. Then she realized that Griselda's hold upon him was much too strong. She was doomed.

"I realize that to remain here is not your wish," Tedric told her. "But I hope you will look upon your stay as an opportunity."

"An opportunity?"

"Yes. You will soon be mistress of this estate. While no one would expect you to begin any of your duties in that capacity while you are ill, your prolonged stay does present a unique situation. You will have a chance to become acquainted with the estate, a chance that otherwise would not have been afforded to a respectable lady such as yourself."

Abigail held back the urge to cringe. Her recent attempts to elope with a man who proved himself a liar were certain to feed the local gossip mill for months, if not years. Was Tedric conveying a hidden message to humiliate her? She narrowed her eyes at her captor.

Tedric cleared his throat. "Since Father was reclusive for such a long time, I am quite sure you know nothing about this property. Why, I doubt before your illness that you had even set foot upon it for many years."

She thought back and discovered her recollections confirmed his speculation. "True. And even so, my memories of that one time are dim. I was still a child. I venture that you and I did not even meet."

"Much to my regret."

His gallant quip caused her anger to evaporate like steam escaping a cup of fresh hot tea. Why did a normal pleasantry cause her to feel so delicious?

"I am just now getting reacquainted with the place myself." He glanced about the room. "I am afraid the years of neglect have taken their toll." Tedric lifted his stare to a chipped piece of crown molding, a look of distress crossing his face. When he sighed and returned his attention to her, Abigail almost felt sorry for him. "You might be aware that illness caused my father to be a recluse during the last years of his life," Tedric informed her. "In his weakened physical condition, he relied on servants to take care of the upkeep. As you can see, their skills and loyalties were limited."

"On the contrary," Abigail interjected, "I found my room quite opulent."

"You are kind." A sad little smile touched his lips. "Now that I am home to stay, I am eager to see the estate returned to its former status." Though the sun had set, Tedric lifted green velvet draperies aside and looked out the window. "You would not remember the gardens."

"What do you mean? There are plenty of gardens here. Missy constantly spoke of all the healing herbs she gathered from them, nursing me when I was sick."

"Yes, we have healing herbs, a few flowers, and fruit trees. And, of course, we have vegetables in summer. But those are necessities. No, what I mean are gardens. Real gardens that would have put Caesar to shame." Tedric returned his stare to the window and began talking, not to Abigail, but to some invisible audience. "When we were boys, my brother and I would run through the maze, playing hide and seek." He paused, a trancelike state suggesting he had ventured well into the past. His voice lowered almost to a whisper. "And later, in those gardens, promenades under the moonlight. . ."

Moonlight promenades? Images of all sorts of beautiful women flooded Abigail's mind. She felt a flush of heat rise from her neck, to her cheeks, to her forehead. Embarrassment had a way of making her turn sanguine. To her further chagrin, she realized that jealousy tempered her emotion. The wretched feeling was most unwelcome.

As though he suddenly realized he had hinted at too much, Tedric spun around and faced Abigail. "In its glory, the Sutton estate was known as a place for conviviality."

"Oh." Whenever she passed the Sutton estate, the house had appeared more intimidating and eerie than hospitable. At that moment, she recalled a legend that the elderly Lord Sutton lived among ghosts who moaned and rattled chains at night. A slight shiver shot up her spine, making her glad she hadn't remembered the ridiculous fable until that moment. She decided not to share the story with her host.

"As you can imagine," he said, "I would like to see our reputation restored."

Abigail nodded despite the fact she couldn't imagine the gloomy old place rocking with laughter, violins playing sprightly music, or the scent of fresh flowers decorating the air.

"I am pleased that you agree," Tedric commented, obviously misinterpreting her nod. "This estate has needed the loving hand of a woman for quite some time. And I have a positive sentiment that you, Miss Pettigrew, will be instrumental in bringing my childhood home back to life."

❧

Tedric watched Abigail as she exited his study. He was grateful that she seemed more reluctant to leave his presence than she had in the first few moments after receiving the letter from her stepmother. Tedric had only briefly met Griselda Pettigrew, and he did not anticipate the inevitable second encounter with pleasure. Rumor had it that she was a woman of questionable pedigree. Her reputation was that of a woman who sought to climb the social ladder and to meet her objective. She was not above enchanting an aging, if somewhat impoverished, member of the aristocracy into marriage.

His thoughts turned, as they so often did, to Abigail. Her honey blond loveliness surely was more than enough to stir insecurities in a confident woman of the world, let alone a woman with such a tenuous hold on her place in society. No wonder Griselda had such little regard for Abigail's feelings. Had he realized the extent of her animosity toward Abigail when he took her to the Pettigrew estate that rainy night, Tedric would have insisted upon seeing Abigail's father rather than following Griselda's counsel.

Somehow, Tedric didn't regret Abigail's time at the estate.

As for Cecil, he would be pleased to find his betrothed ready to become mistress of the manor upon their wedding day. "Perhaps," Tedric muttered, "the Lord in heaven works in mysterious ways."

nine

A fortnight later, Abigail sailed into the library without knocking. She was too frustrated to wait for a better time to speak with Lord Sutton. Each turn of responsibility at the estate presented a new problem. As their first encounter had promised, the housekeeper proved a hard and difficult woman. The conflict with Mrs. Farnsworth caused the rest of the staff to fall into slovenliness. The situation had become too urgent to wait.

Upon entering, she saw Tedric at his desk, poring over a large book. After she reached the halfway mark across the expansive library, she paused in wonder. The book looked much like one her family kept in a treasured place at home. She looked again.

Was Tedric reading his Bible?

She observed him as he read, his study so intent that his lips moved with the words, though she heard no sound. Abigail shook her head in amazement. How could a cad like Tedric be interested in the Bible?

Still, she doubted anyone who gave Christianity only lip service would take time to read the Word, at least not without an audience to appreciate it.

Loathe to interrupt his study, Abigail had just about decided to turn on her heel when he looked up at her. His mouth slackened open upon discovering his visitor, but his eyes held a soft light.

"Abigail." The way his voice brushed over her name sent a wave of pleasure through her.

"Yes," she answered, wishing she could think of a more intriguing answer.

"How long have you been standing there?"

She hesitated. "Less than a moment."

"I beg your pardon." Tedric rose. "Apparently I was so absorbed in my reading that I didn't realize you had entered." His mouth twitched into a frustrated line as he glanced at the open door. "Where is Ralph, I wonder?"

"You gave him the night off. His mother is ill. Remember?"

"Oh yes." He nodded with a few slow motions, a sure indication he barely remembered granting the butler's request. "How does the poor soul fare?"

"She is improving, from what I understand."

"Good. But where is Mrs. Farnsworth?" Tedric looked about the room as though he expected her to materialize.

"Taking her nightly tea, by my leave," Abigail answered. "So." She paused. "Are you reading Scripture?"

He looked down at the book, which was still open on his desk. "Yes. I read it each night about this time."

To her surprise, his voice was soft, as though he were revealing a deep secret. His eyes failed to meet hers.

"I must say I am quite surprised."

He looked up. "Surprised? Pray tell, why?"

"I thought a man like you would have no interest in God's Word."

As soon as her words registered, Tedric winced. She blurted an apology. "I beg your pardon."

"That is quite all right." His lips pouted ever so slightly, and a stricken light entered his eyes, but he didn't prod Abigail for an explanation. "I suppose you could tell from my absorption in my reading that I find the Proverbs fascinating."

"Oh? So do I. What passage are you studying?"

"Are you sincere in your query?"

"I am."

"Very well." Tedric picked up the Bible and read. "Proverbs, the twenty-second chapter, verse twenty-nine. 'Seest thou a man diligent in his business? he shall stand before kings; he shall not stand before mean men.'"

Abigail waited for him to continue reading, but he stopped and shut the book with a soft thud. "That is all? That is the passage you were contemplating so deeply?"

"Is that not enough?"

She thought for a moment, then realized the words were indeed meaty. "Yes, it is."

Abigail restrained herself from leaping with excitement. So, he was interested in the admonitions of Scripture. The man she had been led to believe was a cad, a rake, and a rogue consulted Scripture every night. Her chest heaved once, a natural reaction to the softening of her heart. Perhaps marriage to Tedric wouldn't be such an ordeal after all.

He motioned for her to sit in the stiff chair across from his desk. "What prompts your visit?" His voice was not unkind.

She shook her head. "There is no need to bother you now. What I have to say can wait."

"No. I want to hear you."

Surrendering, Abigail took her seat.

Tedric sat back down and placed his silk-clad elbows on the polished wood. "What brings you to see me at this late hour?"

"Your staff," she informed him.

"My staff?" His dark eyebrows shot up as he set his back against the chair. "Indeed? Are they not satisfactory?"

"Satisfactory? I should say not. They are impossible!" One quick look around the library incited her to further ire. "It is no wonder this place is in a state of disrepair." Abigail wanted to clench her hand into a fist and beat it on the desk, but considering his past observations about her maturity—or lack thereof—she crossed her arms once more, stiffened them across her chest for emphasis, and settled for exhaling with a loud huff.

"I can see they have vexed you greatly. So what is the quandary now, Abigail?" Instead of sharing her irritation, Tedric looked as though he could barely contain a grin.

"Tedric, I do believe you enjoy my misery."

" 'Enjoy' is too strong a word. I do find your antics quite entertaining, however." This time, he didn't bother to conceal his real feelings.

Oh, why did the smile that lined his face have to be so devastating?

She swallowed. Maybe she should reconsider bothering Tedric with all her problems. This was not the first time she had asked him to address a conflict between herself and the servants. Each time she approached Tedric, she sensed she only appeared to be more helpless.

In truth, Abigail was helpless, or at least hapless. Griselda had taught her most of the essentials the position as mistress of a manor held, but her stepmother's skill made the execution of each task seem effortless. Griselda issued a command, and the proper servant rushed to please her. Why couldn't Abigail garner the same response at the Sutton estate?

"The servants just do not seem to listen to me," Abigail confessed.

"How strange." Tedric touched his forefinger to his chin. "I instructed them that they are to carry out your orders. They are fully aware that they can be dismissed if they disobey."

"Not all of them are difficult. Certainly Missy is doing her best," Abigail rushed to clarify. She would always remain loyal to the one maid who had shown faithfulness to her throughout her ordeal. "It is just that, well, Cook does not like the menus I propose, the chambermaid is always late because she persists in flirting with the footman, and the housekeeper refuses to discipline her staff."

Amusement no longer showed itself on Tedric's face. "She has been running the house without interference for so long, I am afraid your presence has caused her not a small amount of resentment. That shall not be tolerated. I will have a talk with her."

"Oh, please do not dismiss her! Why, I have not the faintest idea where I would be without her."

"Bad help is better than no help, then?" he asked.

Abigail sent her gaze to the leather-clad toes just visible beyond the hem of her skirt. "I suppose."

"Well, then. That explains your problem. I think Mrs.

Farnsworth senses your feelings. She believes she will keep her job whether she listens to you or not."

She looked up at Tedric. "Will she?"

"That is for you to decide." He leaned more closely toward Abigail. "Are you certain you would not like to dismiss her?"

She gasped. "Why, I could not possibly."

The shadow of a smile touched his countenance. "Surely you are not afraid of your own housekeeper."

"My housekeeper? On the contrary, she is your housekeeper."

He lifted a forefinger. "She is the Sutton housekeeper. And in only a short while," Tedric added, pointing at her, "you shall be Lady Sutton."

Abigail suddenly became aware of her beating heart. Lady Sutton! The words that once had filled her with dread now held the power to spark happy anticipation.

She let her gaze dart to and from Tedric in a few brief spurts, aware that gazing straight into his eyes would be too bold for a lady. How had she come to this juncture, the point where she looked upon her wedding day with wild anticipation? How had she grown eager to wed a man known to be a cad, a rake, or worse?

Even during the dark hours when she had hated him most, Abigail had always thought Tedric handsome. Even then, when he entered a room, she found herself eager to see him. Now that she had been at the estate for awhile, Abigail's opinion had changed, inch by inch. Lord Sutton was reputed to spend months at a time away on murky business in London. Yet since her arrival, he had not left the estate for any prolonged period of time. Not for business, not for pleasure.

She had been warned that Lord Sutton was bound to take advantage of his betrothed, yet Tedric had never attempted any liberties, a fact that left Abigail feeling a hint of disappointment.

The man in question interrupted her meandering thoughts. "Perhaps after you become Lady Sutton, you shall enjoy the respect you deserve."

"Respect is often given to those not deserving of it. Griselda warranted no respect, yet she commanded absolute obedience." As soon as the words snapped from her lips, Abigail felt the color empty from her face. "Forgive me. I did not mean those words."

"I know you did not mean to say that." Tedric's emphasis on the word say showed her that he realized her true meaning. "I met your stepmother once, only briefly. I assure you, her stature and presence are quite imposing. Methinks I would be afraid of her myself."

Relieved that Tedric was unwilling to upbraid her, Abigail allowed a giggle to escape her lips. "Indeed?" she teased. "Methinks you should be afraid of no one."

"I am certainly not afraid of the housekeeper. I shall dismiss her on a moment's notice if you ask."

"But then we would have no housekeeper at all." Fear showed itself in her shaking voice.

Tedric reached his hands over the desk. Without thinking, Abigail reached for them and allowed Tedric to hold her hands in his. "My dear, sweet Abigail. You need not be so afraid."

Abigail permitted her eyes to fix upon his. For a shining moment, she looked closely enough to observe the gold flecks in his blue irises. Not for the first time, she noticed his smooth face, dotted by miniscule whiskers making their reappearance after a close morning shave. The scent of clean masculine skin dashed with a few sprinkles of bay rum lured her to draw as closely as the large desk allowed. She leaned against it with a vigor that pained her, but she didn't care. Her only desire was to be closer to him.

Obviously sensing her emotions, Tedric leaned in toward her. She found herself wishing she weren't a lady, that she could stand up and lean over the desk, moving her mouth close enough to let him kiss her. These strange emotions, unknown to her before that moment, left her as exhilarated as a long ride on a galloping steed. No wonder so many women had fallen for him.

The thought caused her to jump back. "No!" she shouted.

Tedric's eyes widened to their full extent. His body flinched. He disconnected his hands from hers with such force that his fingernails made light contact with her skin. "Excusez moi!" he murmured.

His French, so popular among the smart set, only served to remind her how much Tedric enjoyed his role as a man of the world. Her anger grew. "Do not touch me ever again!"

She expected him to retort that once they were man and wife, she would not be permitted to issue such edicts. Abigail wasn't sure about the mysteries of marriage. She had only heard whispers about what was expected of a wife. Once, she had eavesdropped on Griselda and one of her older friends. Lady Edith remarked that she survived her wifely obligation by following her own mother's advice to think of one's duty to the Church. What did that mean? Both women turned sanguine and clapped their mouths shut as soon as they realized Abigail had overheard their words.

Hoping to discover the truth, later Abigail inquired, only to endure Griselda's tongue lashing. The reprimand about eavesdropping hadn't been nearly as disturbing—or intriguing—as Abigail's unsatisfied curiosity. What was this awful event that married women were forced to endure? And if it were so awful, how did they manage to survive? She supposed her curiosity would end soon after the wedding ceremony.

Such forbidden thoughts caused her to feel shy. Abigail sent her stare down to a few planks of the floor, its knotted beauty marred by scuffmarks. She resolved to remind Mrs. Farnsworth to have the floors polished.

"I beg your forgiveness, Abigail," Tedric said. "You are right. I should not have touched you. And I will never touch you improperly again."

Her eyes lifted to meet his look. "You shall not?" Why was disappointment granting her an unwelcome visit at this moment?

"No, I shall not." His voice became curt. Tedric's face took on an expression she didn't know, one of a businessman serious about his duties. She wasn't sure she liked it.

"The hour is late," he told her. "Tomorrow morning, prepare a list of duties and present it to Mrs. Farnsworth. Instruct her to put the chambermaid on notice that if her work does not improve, we will no longer require her services. Notify Cook that she is to prepare whatever dishes you suggest as long as the necessary ingredients are available."

Abigail nodded. "May I tell them these are your orders?"

"I would not advise it. If you continue to rely upon my authority, you will never be able to exert your own."

"All right. I will try." Reluctance colored her voice. "But if they resist, I shall tell them you will be most distressed."

"Tell them nothing of the sort." He paused. "I shall be going on business at the close of the week. So I will not be available."

She searched for any signs of sorrow or regret that he would have to leave her. She saw none. Abigail's stomach gave her the undesirable sensation of leaping into her throat. "You will not be here?"

"I shall be in London."

"On business, you say?"

"Yes. On business." His mouth smacked shut.

Abigail wondered what his business was. Even worse, why did his business have to take place in London?

London. The place where Tedric could meet with all the lewd and bawdy women he wanted. Women who already knew everything there was to know about the mysteries of marriage, without the responsibilities. With these types of women, men could forget all about their troubles. They need not vex themselves about the condition of the estate. No lists of duties or meals to plan awaited their approval. They had no need to settle arguments with the housekeeper or cook.

What would it be like to be a woman of ill repute? To be so close to Tedric, to be in his arms for as long as she wanted without a worry in the world? She clenched her hand into a fist when she realized her feelings were those of envy. Envy of brazen, disgraceful women who walked in the flesh. Women who had no idea of God's love for them and had no desire to know Him. Shame filled her being. How could Tedric do that to her?

Tedric arose from his seat, a motion to conclude his meeting with her. Abigail followed suit, averting her eyes.

"Is everything all right, Abigail?" The melody of his voice bespoke compassion.

She nodded.

"Do not be afraid. I will not remain in London for so very long. If you encounter difficulties, you may be assured that I will reprimand anyone who gives you the least bit of trouble. Do you understand?"

She nodded, keeping her focus on the open Bible.

"My dear Abigail, I see how frightened you are. If you were not, you would look at me. If I had the power to send you home until the wedding, I would."

"I know." She brought her gaze to his face. "Your business in London cannot wait?" she ventured.

"I am afraid not. It is quite urgent."

"I understand," she answered, although she didn't.

Terrified of her roiling emotions, Abigail turned and rushed out of the room. She would never let him see her cry.

ten

Though she ran to her bedchamber in tears, Abigail's fit of sadness didn't last long enough for her to don a nightshift.

So Tedric was a believer! A follower of Christ! Or was he?

Eager for warmth against winter's chill, Abigail lunged into bed and threw the coverlet over her head. She sank her cheek into the down pillow. If Tedric were sincere about the Lord, how could he go to London to gamble and meet with women?

"But he never said he was going to see other women or go to the gaming tables," she reminded herself. *Then again, would he?*

"Father in heaven," she petitioned, "I pray that You will lead Tedric away from all temptations while we are apart from one another. Please give me solace while he is gone."

She swallowed. Had she really just sent up a plea expressing regret that Tedric was leaving?

"Lord, is it possible? Could it be Your will for me to marry Tedric after all?"

She wondered how that could be. Just weeks ago, Abigail had been convinced that Henry Hanover was to be her groom. But Henry's wedding to the wealthy London heiress had come and gone.

Abigail knew how wrong she was to pay attention to idle gossip, but when Henry's name was mentioned, she couldn't resist. All reports indicated the wedding day brought about much commotion and excitement in London. The music of Neil Gow's band and tables burdened with exotic fare including sweets from Gunther's resulted in a ballroom overflowing with guests. Abigail could only imagine such a lavish reception.

Envy filled her, until fresh news about the society couple

circulated. Almost as soon as the honeymoon abroad ended, reports about Henry's unfaithfulness to his bride and love for fast city life were bandied about by every tongue in the village. Rumor had it that Henry had already spent a third of the heiress's fortune at the gaming tables. Tongues clucked in sympathy for the heiress, yet expressed no surprise in Henry's behavior.

Abigail shivered, but not from cold since her body heat had permeated the covers. Rather, the chill signaled her fright and remorse over what had almost happened. Abigail pulled the covers down from over her face but kept them over her shoulders.

She sighed. How could she have been so foolish about Henry? He had never loved her at all. Unaccustomed to men of the world, she'd mistaken his flirtations for true romantic interest. Perhaps her rebellious heart and her dislike of Griselda had caused her desire to disobey her father by attempting the failed elopement. True, the Lord had used Henry to humiliate her. Much as she disliked His discipline, she knew it only showed her Savior's love for her.

She thought back to the night Tedric had rescued her. Yes, rescued. Long ago, she had stopped considering the event a kidnapping. Now, Tedric had freed her from a terrible fate. No, two terrible fates. One was the misfortune of becoming Lady Hanover. Her family had little money. That much she knew even though Father tried his best to shield her from the harsh reality. Henry never would have been satisfied with what little dowry she could offer. Again, she felt a twinge of pity for the dowager whose money he ran through like a carefree child sprints through a spring rain.

The second fate from which Tedric rescued her was certain death. Exposure to so much freezing rain and biting wind no doubt would have caused her to cross death's threshold. Perhaps after what she had done to disgrace her father and the family name, she deserved the sting of death. But the Lord had seen fit to let her live. Was Tedric's rescue God's way of showing Abigail the folly of her ways? Was He trying to lead her to the true love He planned for her—a lifetime of love with Tedric?

"Is this why my heart is softening toward him?" She gasped in happiness. "Heavenly Father, if it is so, I rejoice!"

With a swift, eager motion, Abigail sat upright and reached for the Bible on her nightstand. She flipped through the pages just after the book's center. Soon she found the Scriptures she sought, the ones offering advice on how to be the perfect wife. Surely Tedric deserved the perfect wife, or at least a wife as perfect as she could be.

Several times she read Proverbs 31. Her mind lingered on one passage in particular: "Who can find a virtuous woman? for her price is far above rubies. The heart of her husband doth safely trust in her, so that he shall have no need of spoil. She will do him good and not evil all the days of her life. She seeketh wool, and flax, and worketh willingly with her hands."

"Worketh willingly with her hands." She snapped her fingers. "I know! I shall embroider him a handkerchief. One with his initials and a bit of decoration."

But the fabric? She would send Matthew out to the village on the morrow to secure a good square of the finest muslin. And yes, she needed white silk twine. She could borrow a needle from the estate's sewing supplies.

For once, she was grateful to Griselda. "A lady sews a fine stitch," her strict stepmother had repeatedly said while refusing to let Abigail get away with sloppy needlework.

At the time, Abigail had resented Griselda's persnickety demands. Who cared how finely she could darn a stocking, as long as she left no holes? And so what if the French knots on the tablecloth she decorated weren't all the same size and if some were a bit lopsided? Would anyone notice? Griselda thought so, and to prove her point, she forced Abigail to pull out and sew again any stitches that were less than perfect. After much frustration, Abigail had learned to form stitches carefully and correctly on the first attempt. Finally, Abigail could appreciate Griselda, if only for one small detail.

She clasped her hands. Tedric was certain to appreciate the gift she would make for him.

Another idea seized her. She would prepare soaps for him. The ones she had in mind wouldn't be the haphazardly shaped laundry soaps she usually made, but fine soaps, formed well in flawless ovals. She tried to remember the stock of ingredients in the herb house. Had she seen one or two bottles of perfumed oil? Well, if not, she would use whatever herbs she could find to make some. Tedric's soap would be scented with a masculine fragrance, a rich aroma befitting one of his rank and position. She inhaled stark air, but in her mind, the fragrance came to life.

As she closed her Bible, she contemplated other gifts she could present to her betrothed. Her stomach churned with an unpleasant thought. What if Tedric laughed at her gifts? What if he used the fragranced soap to be more attractive to the women in London? What if he showed off the beautifully embroidered handkerchief to the men at the gaming tables, men she imagined too rough and crude to appreciate her work? Would they poke fun at her naïveté? A little girl staying dutifully at home and working to be the perfect wife, while the man she had grown to love with desperation caroused in a distant city, doing as he pleased?

No! She would prove herself far superior to any London trollop, more enchanting than the temptations waiting at any gambling hall. She wasn't sure just how, but certainly if she kept praying, the Lord would show her the way. Suddenly feeling cold prick her flesh again, she dove back under the covers and fell into a fitful sleep.

❧

Tedric tried to concentrate on his Bible but to no avail. Realizing the futility of his efforts, he shut the book. Absently, he ran his hand over the cover that showed marked wear from years of use by the Sutton family. Well, at least some members of the Sutton family.

He sighed. Why couldn't Cecil tear himself away from the gaming tables and immoral women of London? He had a treasure of a woman waiting for him right at home, but he wasn't even willing to journey back long enough to discover the delight that was Abigail Pettigrew. A fortnight ago, Tedric had written, begging Cecil to return home for a few days, at least long enough to form a brief acquaintance with his betrothed. The letter he received in response was curt, except the portion that now led Tedric to make an arduous and unplanned trip to the city.

Tedric reached into the top left-hand drawer, the one where he kept pending correspondence. He extracted the letter and read:

Tedric,

I understand you want me to meet my betrothed, but at this time, returning to the estate does not suit my pleasures. How you can endure remaining in such a dreary place, out in the middle of nowhere, I cannot fathom. In any event, I have more pressing business that needs tending immediately.

My dear brother. . .

Tedric stopped reading for a moment. Whenever Cecil addressed him as such, he could be sure trouble followed. He sighed and returned to the letter.

My dear brother, you must journey here and meet me to aid in settling the business of which I speak. You see, there is a small matter of money. It seems there is a disagreement between myself and the proprietor of one of the establishments here in town. This gentleman claims I owe him a not inconsequential sum of money as a result of a bad run of luck at the gaming tables. I, on the other hand, have no recollection of this matter. He claims that perhaps my memory has been dulled by the ale I consumed that evening. On this matter, our recollections also disagree.

In the meantime, I am enjoying the generous hospitality of one Lizzie Thompson in St. Giles. I assure you that Lizzie is a fine woman indeed, though misunderstood by the wagging tongues about town. I suggest we find some recompense for her as well. After all, she is going to quite some effort to see that my stay here is agreeable.

In the meanwhile, I promised you would be arriving soon to settle this matter. Since I am a longstanding patron of the gentleman's establishment, he has agreed to not take this matter any further for a fortnight. Otherwise, I might be enjoying the hospitality of the constables, which I am quite certain would not meet the expectations or requirements of a gentleman of my stature. However, I understand the constables may be willing to permit me to remain in my current circumstance should they find an extra few pounds in their palms.

I shall be expecting you within the fortnight. You may remember me to my betrothed.

Your loving brother,
Cecil

As he tossed the letter on top of his desk, Tedric wasn't sure whether to spit in contempt or cry out for the lost soul of his brother.

Tedric heaved an exasperated sigh. He had not had occasion to meet the Lizzie Thompson that Cecil mentioned, nor did he seek the opportunity. An image of Lizzie formed in his mind. Cecil was drawn to large, coarse women who wore immodest evening dresses during the day and spoke boldly, using the slack grammar of their class. How could such a woman compare to the spiritual and physical beauty of Abigail?

Abigail, with dark blond locks she had taught Missy to style. Smooth skin, with a touch of pink in each cheek and lips a touch pinker. Abigail's eyes sparkled, but not with suggestion of illicit pleasures. She was much too innocent to lead weak men down that broad road.

No, Abigail was decidedly not the type of woman Cecil admired or sought. Still, how could Cecil be so thoughtless as to make a passing mention of Abigail at the end of this letter, not even writing her name, as though she were a mere fixture in the house rather than the woman he would soon marry? Tedric shrugged. Why even bother to give her such a puny message?

Of course, Cecil had no love for Abigail, a woman he had never met. Tedric suspected Abigail, even in her great artlessness, did not presume Cecil loved her. Tedric doubted that Abigail had even become aware of the ever-absent Cecil until their recent betrothal.

Tedric shook his head when he thought about Abigail's father. How could a loving parent wed his daughter to a man—any man—without at least making sure she had met the man? Tedric drummed his fingers on his desk, observing them as mindlessly as though they belonged to someone else. Perhaps if Cecil had met Abigail, he wouldn't be so eager to stay in London, consuming with his passions whatever remained of the Sutton fortune.

In the meantime, Tedric felt charged with Abigail's safety and reputation as she prepared to be his brother's wife.

His brother's wife. Not his own.

Oh, why did Cecil's betrothed have to be so beautiful? Why couldn't she be an old dowager, like the new Lady Hanover? Or a plain-faced girl? Or maybe even a London sophisticate, though not of a reputation sullied beyond all reason.

As soon as the thoughts entered his mind, Tedric could answer them. Abigail's attraction was her family name. Pettigrew. A name of the local aristocracy not besmirched by any whiff of scandal. The root of local aristocracy, the Pettigrew name was from a heraldic lineage dating back to King James. Pettigrew was the kind of name a man such as Cecil needed if he ever hoped to pull the Sutton name out of the mire into which he had thrown it. Where he most likely would continue to keep it. Lady Abigail would run the estate while her husband played in London most of the year.

And what would Abigail and the Pettigrews receive in return? They would be forever tied by marriage to a name of prestige and its title. Tedric supposed if he were in Lord Pettigrew's position, the marriage would seem a good, if not ideal, match.

What would be the ideal match? The thought pricked his conscience. A rhetorical question, to be sure. No matter how much he felt his love for Abigail grow, she belonged to his brother. He forced himself to ignore the light of love he sensed in her expression, in the wistful way she looked at him. In the way she leaned toward him that very evening, her lavender scent so tantalizing. . .

"No!" The word she had used to stop him from touching his lips to hers arose to his own mouth. He was grateful to the Lord that Abigail was a woman of unblemished character. Otherwise. . .

He couldn't think of that now. Not now. Not ever. Perhaps the trip to London was timed perfectly. Perhaps he could thank the Lord for that small favor.

eleven

A fortnight finally passed. Tedric was due to return! He would be arriving at the estate that day, in fact. As soon as Abigail issued the servants' orders to Mrs. Farnsworth, she lit up to her bedchamber and shut the door behind her. She scurried to the vanity mirror and studied her reflection. Were her cheeks just a touch more rosy than yesterday? Were her eyes just a bit brighter? Perhaps.

No. They definitely were.

Abigail clasped her hands together and lifted them to her heart. How long she had waited for Tedric to return! Even with all the time she'd spent sewing the muslin kerchief for her beloved, the hours, the minutes, the seconds dragged by with the speed of a tortoise.

She placed her hands on her hips and tossed her head back. Mrs. Farnsworth hadn't given her a lick of trouble all the time Tedric had been absent. Could it be she acted as confident as she felt? Could Mrs. Farnsworth have decided that Abigail would indeed be the lady of the manor, a force to be obeyed?

Abigail sent her reflection a nod. The young woman in the mirror nodded back with just as much bravado.

The motion sent honey blond curls flying forth. She tried to blow them back into place, to no avail.

"We cannot have that, now can we?" she asked the other Abigail.

She picked up the silver bell on her nightstand and summoned Missy. Since Abigail remained at the estate, Tedric had allowed her to promote Missy to the position of ladies' maid. The leap for such a young and inexperienced maid didn't suit Mrs. Farnsworth, but Tedric approved, considering Missy's kindness and attentiveness to Abigail during her illness. Over the weeks, Missy had become almost a friend and certainly a confidante.

"Yes, M'lady?" Missy curtsied as soon as she entered the room.

"I would like for you to dress my hair."

Missy unbent her knees and grinned. "I thought as much. Didn't ye see?"

"See what?"

Missy tilted her head toward the fire. "I warmed the iron fer yer hair."

"Excellent. You are becoming quite expert at anticipating my needs, Missy. I am pleased."

Missy's smile stretched from one ear to the other. She curtsied at the compliment. "Thank ye, Miss." She gave Abigail a quick look and then averted her stare to the worn rug. "I never in me dreams thought I'd ever be a lady's maid, 'specially to someone as good as ye."

Abigail smiled at the compliment and took her seat in front of the mirror. "Nothing too fancy, Missy."

"Ye want him to know ye missed him, but not so much that ye spent all day fixin' yer hair, eh, M'lady?"

Abigail saw her reflection blush before she sent her gaze to her lap, covered by a blue morning dress. "You might say something of the sort."

"And what dress will ye be wearin'?"

"What is wrong with this one? My lord favors blue."

"But ye like him, don't ye? At least, that's how it's lookin' to me. And ye know what? I think he looks at ye the same way."

"Missy, you have such a wild imagination." Abigail held back a triumphant smile.

"I should be thinkin' a dress a little more low cut might be nice. One that shows off yer womanhood a tech more." Missy rolled a lock of Abigail's hair around the iron to form a perfect ringlet. "At least, that's how my Jack likes fer me to look."

"I am afraid I shall soon be losing you to the stable boy," Abigail observed. She didn't mind that regret colored her voice.

"Oh no, M'lady. I shall always be here fer ye." Missy pointed the iron toward Abigail's wardrobe closet. "Now about the dress, I'm thinkin' the rose-colored one would get his attention."

"Oh, my! But that dress is for evening. I would never consider wearing it in the morning." She remembered the cut and how Griselda had passed the dress on to her after she had ordered a new one to be made for herself. She decided not to tell Missy that she had never worn the rose-colored frock. Abigail blushed to think how her stepmother, wearing such daring garb, had enchanted her father.

"I know a lady's supposed to be proper in public," Missy answered. "But ye don't have to be around us. We won't say a word."

"Not even Mrs. Farnsworth?" Abigail ventured.

"Oh, who listens to her?"

Abigail chuckled. "As much as I appreciate your advice, Missy, I think I should wear what I have on presently. I hope I do not need to get his attention with anything more revealing, particularly since I shall be the only lady here."

"Oh, that's not what I'm meanin'. I'm meanin'. . ." Missy stopped herself. Her face reddened. "I'm meanin', well, ain't all men alike?"

"I hope not," Abigail burst forth. "I certainly hope not."

At that moment, Abigail heard the whinny of horses and the rhythmic creaking of a carriage. She jumped from her seat, rushed to the window, and drew back the green drapery. "He is here!"

Tedric emerged from the carriage. His step was vigorous as usual, though the pace was a bit slower, indicating the trip had not been entirely pleasant.

"I must see him right away." She turned to the maid. "Missy, where did you put the package I gave you for safekeeping?"

"Right here, M'lady." Missy retrieved from a seldom-used drawer an oval-shaped soap wrapped in the muslin that Abigail had embroidered. "See, I tied it in some of that purple ribbon we had, just like ye asked me."

"Thank you, Missy." Abigail was ready to bound out of the room when Missy's voice stopped her.

"M'lady? Would ye like me to go 'round and see what's afoot? Maybe add some mystery to ye, if ye don't mind me sayin' so."

Abigail thought for a moment. "No, I suppose I do not mind you saying so. All right, then. I shall remain here until you return."

The moments Abigail waited seemed the longest in her life. She tried to read Scripture, but her mind couldn't concentrate on the printed words of wisdom. As soon as she heard Missy's footfalls on the stairs, Abigail shut the Bible and looked up.

"M'lord is takin' tea now. He asked to see ye."

Abigail almost let a squeal escape her lips. "I shall go, then." She glanced at Missy for reassurance. "How do I look?"

Missy smiled. "Like a lady should."

Abigail tried not to run down the winding mahogany steps to meet Tedric. With as much dignity as her excitement would allow her to muster, she walked past the foyer, past the study, and into the parlor where Tedric always took tea.

To her delight, he looked upon her with anticipation as he rose from his seat. "Abigail." His voice was filled with warmth.

"Tedric."

He glided toward her and took her hand in his. Ever so lightly, he brushed it with his lips. Abigail immediately took the seat across from the one where he had been sitting. Otherwise, she feared she would faint dead away.

To her disappointment, Tedric seemed not to be equally affected. "I am pleased that you will be taking tea with me. I am quite famished after the trip."

"I am sure." She took a sip of hot beverage even though her elevated body heat meant that she didn't need the warmth it offered. "I hope your business in London went well."

"As well as could be expected."

Tedric didn't sound too enthusiastic. Perhaps her gifts would cheer him.

She had taken such pains with the soap, procuring the best herbs and spices from the estate's stock. In fact, she had supervised the making of more than one batch. Each used a different combination of scents, with varying degrees of success. Finally, her efforts were rewarded when a masculine but sweet aroma drifted from the fourth pot of soap.

Once she discovered the precise fragrance she wanted to use, she put the servants through several more attempts before they produced a consistency of soap that Abigail could declare suitable for Tedric's personal use. She deemed that the soap should appear a pleasing shade of beige, not the dull color of unadulterated tallow. A creamy texture was essential. When the combination was finally achieved, victory was Abigail's. To assure proper form, she shaped each cake with her own hands. When the soap cakes were ready, she chose the oval closest to perfection to present to her beloved.

The servants scratched their heads as they watched the arduous process. If they wondered why Abigail had ordered them on a soap-making binge and why she was so particular in selecting one perfect bar of soap, they didn't voice their questions. Instead, they dutifully stocked the laundry room and toilette closet with the rejected attempts. As a result of such multiplied efforts, the estate now stockpiled enough soap to see them through the next year.

When she wasn't involved with day-to-day chores of running the estate, she had spent every remaining moment on embroidering the square of muslin for Tedric. The last stitch of the elaborate "S" had been sewn almost at the moment the coach pulled into the drive, but her handiwork proved beautiful to the eye. No matter that she nearly went blind or lost so much sleep that exhaustion threatened. Tedric was worth the effort.

❧

Tedric prayed that Abigail couldn't read his face well enough to see his distress. Finding Cecil had been easy. Getting him into a sober state and out of the arms of the woman he was seeing proved impossible.

Lord, why did You allow this dear, sweet girl before me to become betrothed to my brother? Why not me?

"It is such a lovely day, Tedric," Abigail said. "Will you not take a walk with me in the garden?"

Tedric shivered in spite of the fact he sat before the fire. "Thank you kindly, but I think not today, Abigail. The air is much too frigid."

Her mouth dropped open slightly. "Oh? I find it refreshing."

"Indeed?" Tedric wondered at Abigail. Usually when she entered a room, she ran for the fireplace and hovered beside it. He often watched her alternate between rubbing her palms together so rapidly he wondered why she didn't start her own fire, then running her hands with vigor over the length of her arms. Her attempts to convince him that she suddenly found chilly air appealing left him in doubt. What was the real reason she wanted to walk with him?

He had been in London only a short while, but somehow Abigail seemed to have grown lovelier during his absence. Not that he had been in the company of comparable women. He shivered again, only this time the feeling stemmed from disgust. No surprise, Lizzie spoke to him boldly upon his arrival at her house in London, her loud voice and abundant laugh filling the hall with brash suggestions. He wished he could be generous enough to think she was attractive in her way. He could not. Even partaking a meal of vegetable stew with Cecil and Lizzie had been enough to put a strain on his manners. Between the squalor of the place and the boisterous company, Tedric was all too eager to return home to the peace of the estate. After such an experience, his only desire was to wash himself clean.

He watched Abigail take dainty bites of biscuit. How could Cecil prefer the company of such a woman to that of his genteel betrothed? Once again, Tedric drank in Abigail's genuine beauty. Radiant from the inside out, she made him want to draw closer.

"So you will not be returning to London again soon?" she inquired.

"I think not, thank you." Unwilling to look Abigail in the eye, he busied himself in an imaginary task involving the papers on his desk.

Tedric was grateful that he wouldn't be expected to go into details about his business with a woman. Otherwise, he would be forced to tell her the truth. Tedric's hopes of convincing Cecil to return to the estate, if only for a few days, were dashed as soon as he realized his drunken brother was in no rational mind. Even if Cecil had been approachable, Lizzie never left his side long enough for the brothers to discuss any private matters. As soon as Tedric relinquished to Cecil two hundred pounds, Lizzie reached her hand out to acquire her share.

In the presence of Abigail, Tedric tried not to let his revulsion show. The details of his trip and the confirmation that Cecil's character showed no improvement since the betrothal would only break her heart. He couldn't bear that.

Lucky Cecil. A woman that any man would die for had fallen into his lap, and he didn't even appreciate her. "For he maketh his sun to rise on the evil and on the good, and sendeth rain on the just and on the unjust."

"What was that?" Abigail asked.

Tedric felt his face flush hot. "Nothing."

"It sounded as though you were quoting a verse of Scripture."

He sent her a crooked smile. "Just thinking out loud, I suppose."

"Oh, Tedric, was your trip really as awful as all that?"

"I am afraid it was," he admitted.

"You're home now. You need to take your mind off business."

The moment she placed a hand lightly upon his forearm, a warm wave of pleasure shot through his being. Her touch was so unlike the urgent prodding of Lizzie's.

"Perhaps," he admitted.

"Do come with me into the garden," Abigail suggested. "We still have a bit of sun left before the day ends."

He pulled his arm away, though the motion was not abrupt enough to be rude. "Obviously, you have some purpose for wanting me to go."

"Come with me, and you shall see for yourself."

She extended her hand as if she wanted him to take it. Thinking better of it, he placed his own hands in his pockets.

A disappointed look flashed across her face, but she quickly recovered. The smile she delivered his way seemed to make the room hotter than any flames. Still, he reached for his morning coat on the way to the garden and helped Abigail into her shawl.

As expected, the air that greeted them was brisk. Now Tedric was the one rubbing his arms, while Abigail looked straight into the mild breeze as though she welcomed it. Tedric willed himself to adjust to the wind. Once he did, he realized that the outdoors was as refreshing as she had promised.

"So," he asked after they had walked for a few moments. "What did you want to show me?"

She led him to a nearby spot and pointed to the ground where a purple flower had just sprouted. "The first crocus of the season. Spring shall be here soon."

"I have received word from your father that he will be sending a carriage for you tomorrow so that you can return home to help your stepmother."

She barely nodded, continuing to stare at the crocus. But the light had vanished from her face.

Tedric thought a change of subject might cheer her. "Are you looking forward to the arrival of your sibling?"

"Yes. Who would be so cruel as not to welcome a new little baby?" She looked up at him, her eyes glistening. "I–I shall miss you." Her voice was barely audible.

"Now, now. Enough of that." He knew the expression on his face must reveal how bittersweet he felt about her departure. Bittersweet was the only feeling he allowed himself. He strengthened his voice. "You shall have quite enough of me once the wedding takes place and you return here for good."

Abigail didn't answer. Instead, she turned a most becoming shade of pink.

"I beg your forgiveness. It is not proper for me to speak so freely."

"That is quite all right. After all. . ." She looked down at her feet.

Before he could wonder aloud at her remark, she withdrew a piece of fabric wrapped around something from her pocket and handed it to him.

"What is this?"

"A present. For you."

"For me? But what is the special occasion?"

"Silly goose!" Her laugh was musical, a most enchanting melody. "Am I not permitted to present you with a gift?"

A protest tried to escape his lips.

"After all, you have been so kind to me."

Kind. Yes, he supposed he had been. As kind as he felt was permitted under the circumstances.

"Do you not want to see what your present is?" She bounced up and down like a little girl.

"Of course." He studied the package. Fine cotton muslin was tied with a purple ribbon. The pleasing scent of an herbal mixture wafted toward him. So she had made him a gift. If only he could express how much he appreciated her, but he could not. "You are much too generous, Abigail."

"Indeed? You are the one who has been much too generous to me."

"I am afraid your package is too lovely to open."

She giggled. "Open it anyway. And if you want me to, I'll wrap it up all over again."

He smiled, imagining that she would indeed keep her promise should he ask. He untied the ribbon. Inside was an oval soap. "How charming."

"Smell it."

Complying, he lifted it to his nostrils. "The odor is quite pleasing."

"I made it myself. For you."

"Just for me? I am hardly deserving." He decided to guide the conversation to safer waters. "Did you not make a few cakes for your father as well?"

"And make Griselda jealous? Never!"

He shook his head, wondering at her cavalier attitude. "I thank you. You need not have taken such effort, but I shall take great pleasure in your gift."

"Oh, but that is not all. Did you look at the handkerchief?"

He opened the square and fingered the muslin fabric. "This fabric makes a fine handkerchief. Better to invest in quality than to waste money on cheap goods, I say. I am pleased that you are learning to spend the household budget wisely."

"And not just any handkerchief. Look at it closely."

She took the bar of soap from him. "Unfold it and see for yourself."

Further observation revealed an initial, the letter "S", embroidered in script. "Very good, Abigail. I see you have mastered needlework quite nicely. How long have you been working on this?"

"Ever since you left for London. Night and day, practically." Her pride was obvious.

"Very nice." He handed it back to her.

"But it is for you. For your use."

"Abigail, I am not sure I should accept."

Her crestfallen face revealed her dismay. "It is not good enough?"

"It is better than good enough. It is superbly sewn. I am just not certain I should accept."

"Of course you should accept. Why, I shall be most grieved if you do not." She nodded her head once, showing him she meant her threat.

Unwilling to cause strife with his future sister-in-law over a token gift, Tedric argued no more. He folded the handkerchief in a haphazard fashion and stuffed it in his pocket, along with the scented soap. "Thank you. Night is about to fall. We must be returning to the house." He swept his hand toward the door, motioning for her to walk first.

"Oh." Her voice reminded him of the squeak of a mouse. "Yes, I suppose we should be returning."

The rest of the short distance to the house they spent in silence. Never had there been a more agonizing walk.

twelve

By rote, Abigail managed to display impeccable manners throughout the rest of the evening. As soon as she could make excuses to retire, she took leave of Tedric and exited the study. Once she cleared the door, she tried not to run full speed to her bedchamber. Never could she let on how disappointed she had been by his tepid reaction to her gift.

Almost as soon as the door of the bedchamber shut behind Abigail with a resounding thud, she heard a knock.

"I am indisposed," she told her unwanted visitor.

"It's me, M'lady."

Abigail was in no mood to see Missy, but she didn't have the heart to keep her faithful maid at bay. "Very well, then. Come in."

Missy entered and curtsied. "What vexes ye, M'lady? I heard yer door shut all the way down the hall to my room."

"I did not wake you, did I?"

"Oh, no, Miss. I wasn't asleep."

Abigail composed herself and took her seat at the vanity table. She handed her hairbrush to Missy as though this night were just another ordinary time. "What makes you think something is wrong?"

"I don't know," Missy answered, although Abigail could discern from her tone of voice that her maid was not being completely truthful. "Mebbe it's that ye don't slam yer door in such a fashion when ye're in a good humor, eh?" The maid brushed Abigail's hair with far more concentration than necessary.

"I suppose I have given myself away." Abigail sighed. "You do not believe anyone else heard the door slam, do you?"

"Oh, no, M'lady!" Missy shook her head too rapidly for Abigail to be convinced.

"Whether they did or not, it is too late to remedy the situation now."

"What situation?" Missy's voice held an edge that Abigail didn't like. "Didn't he appreciate the gifts?"

She thought for a moment. She supposed Tedric did appreciate the usefulness of the handkerchief and soap. He certainly hadn't said he didn't like them.

"Yes." Abigail knew her lackluster tone and unsmiling expression revealed her doubt.

"Oh. All is well, then. Things are not as bad as they said." Missy clapped her hand over her lips as though she hoped the action would take back her words.

"Who said what?" Abigail became conscious of her heart beating with the type of fear she hadn't felt since Henry left her standing alone in a frigid drizzle in the dead of night. "Tell me."

"Oh, I don't know, M'lady. Idle gossip never did nobody no good." Missy shook her head back and forth in quick motions.

"What idle gossip? What are they saying in the servants' quarters? Tell me. I want to know." Abigail's voice grew higher in pitch as her demands escalated.

"Oh, M'lady. Ye need pay no never mind to what those old hens say."

"I shall decide the extent of my concern. Tell me. I demand to know." Abigail injected enough authority in her voice to show her serious intent.

"They—Mrs. Farnsworth—well," Missy stopped herself.

"What did Mrs. Farnsworth say? If the housekeeper is gossiping about me right under my own nose, I have a right to know what she is saying."

"I don't know much. Just what I overheard. She was sayin' to the chambermaid that, well. . ." Missy tapped Abigail's brush in her open hand.

"Go on."

"That ye had no business actin' the way ye did. Runnin' after a man like a common, like a common—oh, I can't say it,

M'lady. Please don't make me say it." Missy collapsed on the floor in a heap and began to cry.

Abigail rose from her seat and knelt beside Missy. She placed a consoling hand on her maid's shaking shoulder. "That is quite all right, Missy. You have no control over what the housekeeper says. And in any event, I am dragging it out of you."

"I told her ye're betrothed, but she said that just makes the way ye're behavin' all the worse." Missy wiped her eyes with the back of her hand.

A sense of puzzlement caused Abigail's brain to feel as though it were moving about in circles. "I do not understand. Am I not permitted to present my betrothed with a small token of my affection?"

"I don't see nothin' wrong with it meself, but mebbe she has her own ideas about how a lady's supposed to behave. Or mebbe she just misunderstood what I was tryin' to say."

"Maybe so."

Missy's doe eyes became pleading. "I beg of ye, don't tell nobody I told ye. I don't want Mrs. Farnsworth to know. If she is fired from her position, the rest of the staff will be blamin' me. I'd be an outcast in me own quarters."

"I would not dream of betraying your confidence. You have been loyal to me from the first day we met. Even when I was unspeakably rude, you showed me nothing but kindness."

"Ye weren't yerself, M'lady. Who can be, what with such a cough as you had? Why, ye almost caught yer death." Missy's attempts to console Abigail seemed to give her new resolve. She stood upright. "I wouldn't be payin' no mind to what the housekeeper says. You know Mrs. Farnsworth. She's enough to try the patience of the saints, she is."

"Never you mind, Missy. We shall not have to worry about Mrs. Farnsworth much longer."

"Ye'll be firin' her?" Missy's voice rose with anticipation.

"No. At least, not yet. Do you not remember? We are due at my father's estate tomorrow. My stepmother needs my help."

"Oh, yes. I remember." Missy nodded with little enthusiasm. She looked around the bedchamber. "I shall miss bein' here. It's the only home I've known for the past several years."

"I shall miss it too," Abigail admitted. "We shall return before you know it."

"Yer right, M'lady." Missy pasted a grin on her face. "I'd best be packin' yer trunk, eh?"

"Yes. That would be a good idea." Following Missy's earlier example, Abigail scanned the room. Her quarters at home were less spacious and not nearly as well appointed. But those qualities weren't what she would miss. She would miss, well, she would miss everything.

If only she could believe her own consoling words to her maid. Time would pass, but not soon enough.

❧

The next morning, Abigail's father sent a coach for her. She had not seen her childhood home in months. Emotions roiled in the pit of her belly. Only when the house was in sight did she realize how much she missed her father. Would he forgive her? Ever since she awoke to find herself at the Sutton estate, she had been praying that he could.

She sighed. Her stepmother was another matter. Would she be as disagreeable as always, or would the happy anticipation of a new baby's birth leave her in a better humor?

Abigail's devotional time with the Lord had led her to commit Proverbs 18:24 to memory: "A man that hath friends must show himself friendly: and there is a friend that sticketh closer than a brother."

Abigail wasn't sure she could ever be a friend to her stepmother, but for the sake of the family and for her expected brother or sister, she knew she had to try.

She turned her head to look back with longing in the direction of the Sutton estate, even though the home of the man she loved was long out of her field of vision. She had been away from Tedric less than an hour, and despite her disappointment in his earlier behavior, she wished she could return to him.

If only he loved her in the way she had grown to love him! With reluctance she recalled their good-byes. His terse farewell and unwillingness even to touch her hand left her saddened.

Heavenly Father, she prayed, *please be with me. I want to honor You as I come for a short time to live once again with my father and stepmother. Help me to keep a sweet temper, no matter what I might be feeling inside.*

"My what a grand house!" Missy observed.

Abigail turned to see her maid standing behind her, awestruck by the Pettigrew home. She tried to see the gray stone house through Missy's eyes.

"Really?" she answered. "I cannot imagine why you are so taken by the house. Certainly it is no grander than the Sutton estate."

Abigail surveyed her childhood home yet again. Pettigrew Manor boasted the same number of wings—north, south, east, and west—as the Sutton estate. Missy was not yet able to see that each wing contained fewer rooms. However, Abigail realized the Pettigrews' rooms were often larger and, as a result, Abigail supposed the house itself did appear larger than Sutton Manor.

The Pettigrews' inner courtyard loomed larger, but it held only three modest birdbaths and a small fountain. In contrast, the Suttons had imported fine statuary from Italy. A large fountain attracted attention with its sculpted dolphins surrounding a girl and boy whose water pitchers spilled into the pool. She wondered if Missy's opinion would change once she made the same comparison.

Abigail glanced at the grounds. The gardens and outbuildings were well tended, and the maze of hedges and flowers decorating the side yard was larger and more elaborate than the simple flower garden the Suttons enjoyed, but the outbuildings were smaller and, she knew for a fact, far less well stocked than the Suttons'. Naturally, the Suttons owned the grandest stables and largest pastures in the parish, since a portion of their income was derived from horse breeding.

"I should surmise this estate is quite less grand than the Suttons'," Abigail concluded. An unwanted prick of conscience attacked as she realized she should not have been making comparisons between her home and the one she would soon occupy. Had she really once called the Sutton estate gloomy, eerie, and a monstrosity? How far she had come, to now consider her beloved childhood home a place to visit, and the strange house she once hated to be her home.

"But it is grand enough, M'lady. I shall be honored to work here as your maid."

"Yes," she agreed in an attempt to amend her previous observation, "this house is grand enough."

They were just starting up the walk when Father bounded out of the front entrance and rushed to meet Abigail. He looked no different than he had on the night she had left to elope with Henry. The memory sent a shudder down her spine, causing her to refrain from rushing into his arms.

"Abigail! My little Abigail." He held her close. "I have missed you."

"And I have missed you, Father." She broke the embrace and looked deep into his eyes. "So why did you not visit or at least write?"

He turned his face away from her and cast his gaze upon the ground. "Griselda thought it best to let you think about what you had done."

Abigail cringed. Griselda's punishment was harsh, much harsher than she would have given her own daughter. Father's obvious distress willed her to ignore her argument with her stepmother.

"Oh, Father," she said aloud. "I did little but think of how I nearly caused our whole family to be disgraced. I beg your forgiveness."

Her reward was a loving light in Father's eyes.

"I promise never to hurt you in such a manner again. Ever." She curtsied.

"Your apology is accepted." He took her hand in his.

"Come in, my dearest. Welcome home."

His words caused the anxiety she had felt about reuniting with her father to melt. Apparently, the passage of time had served to heal the wound her conduct had left. With an inaudible sigh, Abigail kept her hand in his as they entered the house.

Her happiness was short lived. All too soon he led her to the parlor, where Griselda awaited.

"Abigail, it is so good to have you here again." The smile on Griselda's face conveyed sincerity. Abigail wasn't surprised to see her occupying Father's chair, the most comfortable in the house. Positioned near the fire, she wore a blanket.

"It is good to be back."

"Forgive me for not rising from my seat."

"Certainly. I should not expect that of you." Out of propriety, Abigail didn't refer to her stepmother's delicate condition.

"All of us have missed you beyond words," Griselda said. "I want you to know I have eagerly awaited your return with all my heart."

"You have?" Abigail knew her bulging eyes conveyed her astonishment.

"Yes, I have."

Abigail observed her stepmother. Her extended belly indicated that she was well along toward the time when the birth was expected.

"Thank you." For Father's sake, Abigail tried not to grimace or otherwise let on that Griselda's warm welcome shocked her to the core. The stepmother who in the past had delighted in making her miserable now seemed to be a different person.

"We truly have missed you," Father assured. He put his arms around her. Abigail returned his embrace.

"Dinner will be served soon," Griselda informed her.

Abigail noted the time on the mantle clock. "I am not hungry yet. Dinner is served at a later hour at the Sutton estate."

"Oh, so you already are accustomed to getting your own way at the Suttons'?" Griselda's tone, which had been warm only moments before, now held an edge. "You may indispose yourself at dinner here if you choose, but the meal will not be served a second time."

I should have known her conviviality wouldn't last long.

Abigail pressed her tongue to the roof of her mouth in a physical effort not to lash back. "I beg your pardon, Griselda—I mean, Mother."

She nearly choked on the word. Since living at the Sutton estate, Abigail hadn't thought of Griselda by the name her father preferred. She had forgotten how difficult calling her stepmother by the fond moniker had been. She swallowed before continuing. "I meant no disrespect. Of course, this is my father's house, and while I remain here, I shall obey the schedule set forth."

"Very well." Griselda sniffed.

Abigail cut her gaze to Father. His approving look and slight nod were her reward.

"Abigail, would you fetch me a cup of tea before dinner?" Griselda asked. "I do believe my stomach feels a bit queer."

Father rushed to her side and knelt by the chair. "Darling, are you quite certain you are well?"

"Oh, yes. Quite well." She patted his hand that rested on the arm of the chair. "I just desire a bit of warm tea, that is all. Then my stomach will feel perfectly fine again."

"If I might speak," Missy intervened.

Abigail had been so absorbed in reuniting with her father and facing her stepmother that she had forgotten about poor little Missy. All this time, Missy had been standing in the background, well behind her mistress, blending in with the wallpaper as was expected of a ladies' maid who had not yet been shown to her new quarters.

Abigail motioned for Missy to come forth. As the maid curtsied, Abigail introduced her.

"This is your ladies' maid?" Griselda's eyebrows shot up, bespeaking her doubt.

"Yes. Tedric gave her to me."

"Tedric?" Griselda asked. "Is it not quite familiar of you to refer to him by his Christian name?"

"Griselda, Dear," Father answered his wife, "perhaps we should be grateful that our daughter is getting along so well at the Sutton estate."

"Perhaps." Griselda sniffled into her lace kerchief. "Now about my tea. . ."

"M'lady," Missy said to Griselda with a curtsy, "I should be most honored to fetch it fer ye."

"I think not. I shall trust your mistress to bring me my tea." Griselda turned her face back toward the fire and let out a huff.

Missy nodded and stepped back. Her head was bent downward to the extent that Abigail wondered if her neck would snap.

"You need not speak to my maid in that manner, Mother," Abigail said. "If anyone is to reprimand her, I shall be that person."

"Oh, indeed? I see you have acquired a quite superior attitude during your absence, Abigail." Griselda looked Abigail straight in the eye. "Perhaps your manners shall improve upon your stay here with us. Now about my tea. . ."

Father rose from his knees. Standing beside Griselda's chair, he intervened. "Griselda, Dear, why not allow Abigail's maid to bring your tea? Then you could hear about Abigail's stay at the Sutton estate. It has been so long since she was home. I should like to converse with her for a time."

"I suppose I could ring for Mattie, but I know she is busy preparing pheasant and Swedish turnips for dinner," Griselda objected.

"That is quite all right, Father," Abigail answered. "It would pleasure me to bring my stepmother a cup of tea. Perhaps my maid can be shown to her quarters here."

As Father nodded, she placed a hand on his shoulder, noticing that his features softened with gratitude for her gesture.

"Thank you, my dear," he said. "Though I do want to hear

about your stay at Sutton Manor."

"We will have plenty of time for discourse over the evening meal. I shall eat very slowly. You know how I adore pheasant, especially the way Mattie prepares it."

"How well we all know. Mattie wanted to prepare a special dish for you. Obviously, she has succeeded." A smile filled Father's face.

"Yes, we have made quite an effort for the prodigal daughter," Griselda noted.

"I am not a prodigal. If you will remember, I was forbidden to come back home," Abigail snapped in spite of her earlier resolution to be agreeable.

"Only for the sake of the baby," Griselda argued. "Apparently you do not understand that being exposed to your illness might have put me in jeopardy."

"Yes, Abigail," Father confirmed. "Had you not been ill, we would have welcomed you with open arms."

Abigail bristled but resisted the temptation to comment. Certainly Father would have welcomed her, but Griselda still considered her nothing more than an inconvenience—unless she could be forced to serve her needs.

Griselda nonetheless joined the subterfuge. "Yes, we would have welcomed you, in spite of your blatant disobedience and your ill regard for this family, as you so aptly demonstrated by disobeying your father in such a bold manner. You are lucky he will even permit you in this house after what you tried to do."

"Now, Griselda, you must not upset yourself," Father said, patting her on the shoulder.

"I care not what you say or think. Abigail does not deserve your—or any other Pettigrew's—forgiveness," Griselda snapped.

"I am the master of this house and Abigail's father. I shall be the judge of whether or not she is forgiven. In fact, she has already asked and I have granted her pardon. The topic shall not be revisited." How Father managed to be authoritative and calm at once, Abigail never knew. Yet his words quieted Griselda.

They assuaged Abigail too. She wanted to bite back, but she remembered her quiet time with the Lord the previous night as she had prepared for her return. For her reading, she had chosen another portion of the passage in the fifth chapter of Matthew that Tedric had mentioned: " 'For if ye love them which love you, what reward have ye? do not even the publicans the same? And if ye salute your brethren only, what do ye more than others? do not even the publicans so? Be ye therefore perfect, even as your Father which is in heaven is perfect.' "

She knew perfection could not be achieved in this life except by the Lord Himself. But she could try. *Father in heaven, please forgive me.*

Her sense of mission renewed, Abigail rushed to the kitchen for a cup of tea. Making her way through the hall, she mentally chastised herself. She had barely taken off her cloak and already she was at odds with Griselda. "Father in heaven," she whispered, "why must getting along with Griselda be so hard?"

Mattie interrupted her conversation with the Lord. "Abigail! So good to have ye back home where ye belong. I'm makin' yer favorite dish."

Abigail sent her a hearty smile. "So I heard. Thank you."

"Is Lord Pettigrew with ye?"

"Why, no."

"Oh. I thought I heard ye mumblin." Standing near abundant flames, Mattie wiped her brow with the back of her forearm. She paused, a sure sign that she expected Abigail to respond. "Did ye say somethin'?"

"Oh, nothing," Abigail complied.

"I knows better than that," Mattie said. "But I won't pry none. 'Ceptin' I'm sure if ye got a trouble, it's because of yer stepmother. Am I right in me thinkin'?"

Abigail let out a chuckle in spite of herself.

"See?" Mattie gave a knowing nod. "I've known ye since ye were a wee little girl." She stooped down and placed her palm downward at her knees, showing Abigail just how tall she had been when they first made each other's acquaintance. "And I know yer stepmother." Mattie rolled her eyes skyward. She didn't need to say more.

A chuckle escaped Abigail's throat, filling the kitchen.

"Aye, that's a good sound. One I've been a'missin'. Now what can I do fer ye?"

"I should like a cup of tea, please."

"Let me fetch it right away."

"No, it is for Griselda, I mean, Mother."

"Aye, so she's puttin' ye straight to work, is she?" Mattie shrugged. " 'Tis no surprise." She sent Abigail a look of sympathy. "I'm proud of yer cheerful countenance, my girl. A lesser young woman woulda been poutin' and complainin'."

"Thank you." Abigail sent Mattie a grateful smile to show how much her encouragement was appreciated. She could only pray that over the next few weeks, she could live up to Mattie's praise.

thirteen

"Abigail!" Griselda called. The vigorous ringing of her silver bell followed.

Since she had arrived home, Abigail had grown to despise the sound of that bell. Griselda's summons didn't surprise Abigail. At the stroke of six each morning, her stepmother commenced with her demands. Abigail wondered why she didn't rest as would be expected of a woman in her condition instead of rising so early.

She muttered a prayer for strength and hurried into her stepmother's bedchamber. Griselda sat upright in bed, huddled underneath a pile of covers.

"Yes, Mother?" The word appeared to fall with ease on her lips since the need to use it had arisen often since she arrived home. She felt herself wince all the same.

Griselda nodded toward the fireplace. "Why do you not start the fire anew earlier in the morning? The chill of night is still upon us. It is not nearly warm enough to keep a body from frostbite."

"Really? I do not feel the least bit cold. Perhaps the warmth of my flesh is a result of my movement as I work."

"It is about time you discovered firsthand the rigors of honest work rather than whiling away all of your leisure time writing nonsense in your diary."

Abigail regretted her words even before Griselda's retort. How could she expect a woman well along toward the time of her baby's birth to work with the diligence she, a lithe young woman, could display? As for nonsense appearing in her journal, she could ignore such an insult.

"My apologies. I beg your forgiveness, Mother." Abigail tried to smile over gritted teeth. "I suppose we should instruct the housekeeper to hire a new chambermaid to take over my duties after the wedding."

The wedding. The day she had once anticipated with glee had once again become a time of dread since Tedric now paid her little attention. As she did often, Abigail placed a hand on top of the letter in her pocket, the one letter Tedric had sent during the past month. She supposed she should be grateful for that much, considering his indifferent reaction to her gifts.

Keeping her hand upon the thick paper was enough. Abigail didn't need to look at it. She had memorized every word. To her dismay, Tedric wrote not an apology for his coldness to her before her departure from the Sutton estate, nor of his unremitting love for her. He wrote merely to tell her he was going back to London on business.

Business. What business? Was his business just an excuse to see another woman? A woman who was wiser, prettier, and more sophisticated than Abigail could ever aspire to be? A woman who could offer much more than she, a little country mouse in comparison, ever could?

And to think she had come to trust that Tedric was a believer, a Christian man!

But he was still a man. Griselda often said that all men were alike. Surely Abigail's own father. . .

No. Her stepmother seldom spoke wisely. Why should Abigail believe her admonitions about men and, most especially, about her own Tedric?

"Abigail." Griselda's grating voice interrupted her musings. "You know very well we cannot afford a new chambermaid at the moment. I do not understand why you refuse to let Missy take on more of the duties."

"Missy is already working day and night as it is."

"What occupies her at this moment, pray tell?"

"Emptying the chamber pots." Abigail grimaced. At least she was spared that indignity.

Griselda cut her glance to her own chamber pot.

"She emptied yours before you awoke," Abigail responded

to her unspoken question.

"Excellent. And after that?"

"She will set about polishing the parlor floor."

Griselda raised a forefinger and shook it at Abigail. "Be certain she beats the rug before she lays it back down again. And have her beat it long and well. I do not approve of an indifferent approach to housecleaning."

"I am aware of your feelings concerning cleanliness," Abigail said.

"What will occupy her after that?"

"She is working very hard," Abigail explained. "You must understand that the work is quite a descent for her after she had enjoyed the position of my ladies' maid previously. So you see, I cannot in good conscience ask her to do more."

"So you say. You might not be so generous if we reach the point where we are forced to let the staff go and reduce ourselves merely to a maid-of-all-work."

"I do not think our situation has deteriorated to that extent," Abigail protested.

"Perhaps it does not seem that way now, but remember, we will be needing a wet nurse and a nanny soon." She patted her belly, which protruded more each day. "Your part of the Sutton fortune must be realized soon if we are to continue to live graciously."

"That is all Lord Sutton is to you? A way to get your hands on more money?"

"Do not judge me." Griselda's look pierced Abigail through to her soul. "If you think you are any more to Lord Sutton than a family name and breeding mare, you are a fool."

"I beg your pardon!"

"It is true." Griselda leaned forward as though she was about to reveal a secret. "He has been in London on business quite awhile now."

She wished she could dispute her stepmother's words, but the letter in her pocket confirmed that Tedric was indeed in London.

"I have heard from reliable sources that the rumors about Lord Sutton are true," Griselda elaborated.

Abigail swallowed. "Are those old rumors still circulating?" she asked.

"Unfortunately, more news continues to be added to the old, and nothing changes," Griselda said. "Your betrothed may accomplish a few errands during his trips to London, but he carouses as well. He is known to frequent the gambling halls and is often seen with women of ill repute."

Abigail searched for signs of sympathy in Griselda's face, but her jaw only tightened. "You take great pleasure in telling me this, do you not?"

"Why would I take pleasure in what is only my obligation? As your stepmother, it is also my duty to tell you not to expect his behavior to improve after the wedding day."

"Then everyone will talk behind my back and whisper about me whenever they see me. I shall live my life as a laughingstock." The realization weakened Abigail's voice.

"Not necessarily." Griselda paused. "There is a revenge of sorts that is open to you."

"Revenge? But revenge is the Lord God's."

Griselda let out a world-weary sigh. "Then call it liberty." She set her gaze on Abigail. "Must I elaborate, or are you able to discern what your options might be?"

Abigail thought for a moment. "Perhaps some women might spend an excessive amount of money on party dresses and give fancy balls, but that would give me no satisfaction."

"But something else will." Griselda leaned toward Abigail and crooked her finger, motioning her to come closer. Abigail obeyed. Griselda whispered, "Once they have provided their husbands with heirs, women in similar positions have been known to take a lover."

Abigail stepped back and gasped aloud. "A lover!" she shrieked.

"Quiet! Do you want Missy or your father to come running in?"

Abigail shook her head. Certainly not! The thought of what Griselda had suggested sickened her. "Why, that would be breaking God's commandments!"

Griselda shrugged. "Consider yourself fortunate. Your father made a good match for you, one that will bring you wealth, comfort, and ease. You will never have to worry about money as I do."

"Have our finances truly declined so? Or do you exaggerate to frighten me?"

"I do not exaggerate. If we do not acquire more money soon, I am afraid we might land on Queer Street with the homeless and destitute."

"Then it would seem to me that you would welcome the day of my marriage." Abigail decided not to await Griselda's response. Instead, she grasped for another subject. "Might I bring you hot tea? Perhaps that will warm you."

"Very well."

Eager to leave Griselda's presence, Abigail made her way down the long corridor to the kitchen. Her thoughts wandered to the day in question, her wedding day.

What Griselda said couldn't be true. Or was it? Why would Tedric seem to be one man when he was with her, then another man entirely once the tip of his shoe hit London's streets?

The unwelcome memory of his return to the estate pricked her mind and refused to leave. Tedric hadn't acted like a man in love when he accepted the gifts she had labored so long to craft for him. Over and over, she had replayed the walk in the garden through her mind. Over and over, she had tried to explain away his indifference.

She had made herself believe that Tedric was merely saving his hot emotions for after the wedding, as a gentleman should. She had convinced herself, being aware of her inexperience with men and their ways, that he didn't want to frighten her with any display of the passion to come. Griselda's words made her realize that she had woven an elaborate fantasy for herself. Tedric didn't love her at all. *Why, right this very instant, he is likely in the arms of another woman. . . .*

Abigail forced the image from her mind's eye. She preferred to think about the times they spent together. She had fallen in love with him. She thought he returned her feelings. When she stole a glance at him, she was certain she could see traces of love in his eyes. Or at least a deep fondness. When he was near and his fingers brushed against hers ever so lightly, had those times been accidental? She had not thought so at the time.

So why hadn't Tedric visited? Why had his lone letter been a brief message to inform her of his departure for London yet again?

Her thoughts turned bitter. When she left the Sutton estate, she had consoled herself with thoughts of Tedric's letters. She'd imagined little envelopes sealed in wax with the Sutton family crest arriving with frequency at the Pettigrew estate. Abigail had surmised she would come to know the Sutton footman by sight, that she would anticipate the sound of his horse's trot as yet another letter proclaiming Tedric's undying love was delivered. Certainly the words Tedric could not express when they were face to face could be written in a fine hand. Once she received such a letter, she pictured herself reading it over and over. She imagined herself memorizing each word of love.

But alas, Tedric saw fit to leave her wondering. Wondering what he was really doing in London. Wondering if he could ever love her. Wondering if Griselda's words were true.

So engrossed was Abigail in procuring the tea that, before she knew it, she had completed her task and stood in front of her stepmother once again.

"My, but you dawdle, Child." Griselda extended her hand for the tea.

Abigail chose to ignore her remark. "I added plenty of sugar and cream, as you like."

Griselda tasted the beverage, then grimaced. "This is much too cold. How do you expect this to warm me? Are you determined that I shall catch my death of cold?"

"Why, no. Of course not. Shall I bring you a fresh cup?"

Griselda nodded as she handed the rejected cup back to Abigail. "And make sure it is hot this time."

"Yes, Mother."

"And by the way." Griselda paused, obviously expecting Abigail to turn and face her.

She complied. "Yes?"

"Do not neglect to change the water in the basin. And be certain the perfume jar is filled with lavender water. You tend to let it get too low for my tastes."

"Yes, Mother."

Abigail shut the door behind her. *Lord, why must I serve Griselda? It is difficult enough to call her 'Mother,' but must she treat me like a servant? I know she is taking advantage of her state to cause me to work for her as much as possible. She knows Father would not be willing to stop her. Must I pamper her, Lord?*

Abigail waited for an answer of no to resound from the heavens.

It was not to be.

Abigail paused in the hallway. She had committed a passage from the ninth chapter of 2 Corinthians to memory, one that helped her keep her sanity as she coped with Griselda. "Every man according as he purposeth in his heart, so let him give; not grudgingly, or of necessity: for God loveth a cheerful giver. And God is able to make all grace abound toward you; that ye, always having all sufficiency in all things, may abound to every good work."

"Lord," she added in a whisper, "I know You tell us to pray for our enemies. Well, I am praying now for my stepmother. Surely that is all You expect of me."

No.

No? Had she heard right? Why was it when she wanted the Lord to say no, He remained mute? But when that word was the last she wanted to hear, He spoke as plainly as if He had sent the angel Gabriel to tell her so.

What must she do now? Abigail felt sure that the Lord wasn't asking her to do more work for Griselda. For Father's sake, she had done her best to meet Griselda's requirements, be they reasonable or not. Then what?

No answer followed, but a sense that He would lead her drove her straight to Griselda's side.

"Here is a fresh cup of tea." Abigail set the small tray on the nightstand. "I hope it proves satisfactory this time."

Griselda took a sip. "Yes, this is much better. Thank you."

"Cook said that breakfast will be up shortly."

"Good. I am rather hungry."

Abigail set about lighting the fire. She felt Griselda watching her.

"Abigail?" she ventured.

"Yes?"

Griselda set down her cup. "I want you to know that I am truly sorry for what I had to tell you just now about your betrothed."

"If you are truly sorry, then why did you tell me?"

"As I said, it is my duty as your stepmother. I know you well enough to realize that you have hardly had any exposure to men at all." Griselda paused. "I suspect no one has even so much as kissed you under the Christmas mistletoe."

Abigail didn't bother to conceal her shock. "Of course not! Why, I would not permit such a thing!"

Griselda nodded. "Or rather, in light of your plain appearance, no man ever made the attempt."

Abigail wanted to defend herself. Unable to think of a time when a man had sought her attentions with ardor, she remained mute.

"Not to mention, you still spend far too much time writing in that diary of yours. If you had socialized instead of seeking solitude, popularity would not have eluded you."

"I hardly write in my diary at all now," Abigail murmured.

"Good. You should have abandoned that childish habit years ago. But perhaps it is just as well that you remained so pure,"

Griselda said. "Your innocence is one of the reasons why I believe Lord Sutton was willing to agree to the betrothal. Despite his abominable behavior with other women, he would, of course, want his own wife to be pure."

"To be sure." Abigail couldn't dispute Griselda's wisdom. She ignored the queasy feeling that arose in her midsection.

"You should be thanking me for my counsel, as painful as it may be," Griselda said. "Some stepmothers, and mothers, for that matter, would let you walk down the aisle without a single word indicating what to expect. But not I. Since the betrothal is already arranged, you must make the best of it. But of course, you have much to gain. There is much to be said about the power and prestige of bearing the Sutton name."

Abigail nodded weakly. Power and prestige were not her desires, but if they were to be thrust upon her, she would do with them what God willed.

"Enough of that." Griselda turned her tone light. "I am wondering, did I miss the evening mail yesterday?"

"No, Mother. There was nothing for you."

"Oh." Griselda looked much too engrossed in her tea.

"Were you expecting a letter?" Abigail ventured.

Griselda shrugged. "I was rather hoping. . .well, I was thinking perhaps my sister in Dover would write me a line or two. She knows how lonely it is out here in the country."

"Perhaps a letter will arrive for you today." Even Abigail was shocked by the sympathy her own voice held. Then she remembered when she was bedridden with no one to talk to but Missy. "I should think you would have plenty of company. Father dotes on you."

"Yes, he is kind. But it is not the same. I miss the parties and balls we had at home," Griselda confessed.

"As if you would be permitted to attend in your delicate condition."

"True enough." Griselda looked down at her expanded midriff. "I look forward to the day the baby arrives."

"As do we all." Abigail studied her stepmother. Where once

she had been youthful and lively, the expectation of birth seemed to have taken its toll. She looked bloated and tired. Earlier her father had been able to bring a chuckle to Griselda's lips, but Abigail couldn't remember the last time she had seen her stepmother so much as smile. How lonely she must be, rarely leaving her bedchamber. The realization caused her to pity Griselda. "I cannot hold a ball here for you, but maybe I can be a little bit of company. Would you like for me to linger awhile?"

"Does time permit?"

"If you say it does. I know there is work to be done."

"Perhaps you should go about that, then." Griselda stared into the fire, but her eyes took on a glossy cast as though she didn't really see the flickering flames.

"I think I might spare a few moments." Abigail consulted the clock. "The time has come when I usually spend a few minutes with the Lord."

"Really?"

"If you like, we can share the passage I have planned for today."

Griselda nodded. Abigail sensed that her eagerness for devotions stemmed more from loneliness than the desire to draw closer to the Savior, but she felt a strong leading to share her time with Griselda.

Abigail took the chair beside Griselda's bed.

Griselda handed her a Bible. "What passage are you reading today?"

She opened the book to the sixth chapter of 1 Timothy and read the tenth and eleventh verses: " 'For the love of money is the root of all evil: which while some coveted after, they have erred from the faith, and pierced themselves through with many sorrows. But thou, O man of God, flee these things; and follow after righteousness, godliness, faith, love, patience, meekness.' "

"Did you select that passage just to torment me?" Griselda asked.

"Why, whatever do you mean, Mother dear?" Abigail couldn't resist teasing.

"That is not a very long passage," she scolded.

"But surely there is enough meat to chew on."

"Indeed," Griselda answered, and launched into her thoughts on the verses.

As they studied together, Abigail and Griselda shared their thoughts as equals. The realization that Griselda had far more worries than Abigail had imagined struck her. Perhaps her stepmother wasn't so evil, after all. Perhaps she wasn't put on earth solely to plague her innocent stepdaughter.

Before they realized how much time had flown by, Missy entered the room with Griselda's breakfast tray. "My, my. I never thought I'd see the day. . . ."

"When the Lord works, you never know what He might show you," Abigail answered.

"She is right," Griselda agreed.

"I suppose this concludes our study. Do you want to pursue more tomorrow?" Abigail asked.

"If you will allow me to select the verse."

"All right."

"Oh, Abigail," Griselda said as her stepdaughter tried to exit the room.

"Yes?"

"Do remember to fetch me the newspaper, will you?"

"Yes, Mother."

Missy giggled as she shut the door behind them. "Ye didn't think she'd change her temperament completely in the space of an hour, did ye?"

"I suppose not," Abigail agreed. "But I can see now, the Lord has changed much harder hearts than hers."

But would He change Tedric's? She prayed He would find a way.

fourteen

As the coach made its way back home from London, Tedric looked at his sleeping brother. Cecil's mouth opened and shut with the rhythm of each snore. Drool slithered from the corner of his lips. Tedric scrunched his nose in disgust. Nevertheless, he found his kerchief and wiped his brother's lips before the liquid could drip onto the floor.

Tedric balled up the old square of cotton so the wet portion remained unto itself, touching neither his fingers nor his woolen traveling suit. Wrinkling his nose, he jammed the offending cloth back into his pocket.

Tedric was grateful he had a well-worn kerchief on hand for such an occasion. He wondered if Abigail had embroidered a decorative "S" on a square of muslin for Cecil and if that particular piece of her handiwork would be used for such a disgusting purpose. He hoped not. Abigail's efforts were much too precious.

Tedric glanced at his sleeping brother once more. Certainly Abigail deserved better than the future that awaited her with Cecil. But he could ill afford to concern himself with that. His destiny was to be her brother-in-law, not her husband. To encourage any party involved to dissolve the betrothal would bring disgrace upon the Sutton name. Even worse, such action could only lead to the revelation of his own shameful ulterior motive for wanting to stop the wedding—his own desire for Abigail.

So why did he dwell upon Abigail's fate?

Watching his brother in repose, Tedric wondered how Cecil could slumber as the coach hit rut after rut in the road. Then again, the four pints of lager he'd consumed at breakfast along with his customary three eggs and pork pie could have acted as a powerful sedative.

Tedric suspected he should be grateful for his brother's slumber. As long as he slept, Cecil wouldn't argue, or worse, try to escape. Tedric wished he could have convinced Cecil to return home long enough to see Abigail without resorting to threats and promises. Cecil had agreed to the betrothal of his own free will. The least he could do was to visit his intended long enough to set the date and make arrangements for proper prenuptial entertaining.

Had Cecil returned when Tedric first asked on his previous visit to London, Abigail would be Cecil's wife by now. She would not have been forced to return to the Pettigrew estate to help her intimidating stepmother. But Cecil's reticence to leave the city left Tedric no alternative but to send Abigail home since she had recovered from her illness and Griselda beckoned. For Abigail's sake, he wished he could have kept her at the Sutton estate. Tedric suspected that love and altruism were not Griselda's motivations for wishing her stepdaughter's return.

Cecil flipped over in his sleep, punctuating the movement with a loud snort. Tedric reminded himself to be certain that Abigail could enjoy private quarters for sleep, lest Cecil keep her awake all night. He imagined gentle Abigail's shock upon spending time in close proximity to Cecil. Tedric supposed Cecil was charming in his way, but. . .

If only he could have changed places with his brother!

Tedric imagined a reversal of circumstance. If he were the one betrothed to Abigail, he would have been free to reveal his heart. Upon his last correspondence, he could have written how he really felt about her, the love he held for her, the love that consumed his thoughts. Instead, he confined himself to one letter. Even then, he sent only to convey urgent news. He struggled to keep the contents of the message appropriate between a man and his brother's future wife rather than that of a besotted lover to his beloved.

Tedric's mind returned to the last day he had seen her, the

day she'd presented him with gifts she had fashioned with her own hands. After many uses, the soap Abigail had created for him was almost gone. He had given in to the temptation to hold onto a sliver so he could still enjoy the fragrance every now and again.

He reached into the pocket of his vest and fingered the handkerchief Abigail had embroidered just for him. Often during the day, he would take out the muslin square and look at it, studying Abigail's fine needlework. From all appearances, the poor girl had spent hours on the elaborate initial, sewing countless decorative stitches on each side.

When she had given him these tokens of friendship, propriety demanded that Tedric not respond with glee. He would always remember the way her mouth had slackened and her eyes had grown moist with unhappy teardrops when he unceremoniously stuffed the soap and kerchief in his pocket and ended the walk in the garden.

He looked upon his brother once again. Cecil's paunch, which made him look older than his thirty years, hung over the edge of the seat. Years of hard drinking had left his face puffy and his round nose veined in red. Hair that had once been lustrous and thick had thinned with age, though Cecil still succeeded in concealing his bare scalp with the remaining locks.

Tedric knew why Cecil was popular among his friends at the gaming tables. Always quick to place a bet, Cecil was a cavalier loser. When he did win, he never failed to buy a round of ale for his cohorts in celebration.

Women were another matter. Tedric wondered what members of the fairer sex saw when they looked at Cecil. Just as quickly, he realized he knew the answer. They saw a flirtatious, vibrant, and rich man. Portliness to them bespoke prosperity. His protruding belly and fleshy hands told them that Cecil never needed to worry about where he would find his next meal, nor did he need to work long and hard to procure the finest fare. Cecil's clothing, a wardrobe of fashionable suits tailored in the finest cloth, confirmed this deduction by screaming his aristocratic roots.

Tedric wondered how many women in the past had pinned their hopes on Cecil, only to be disappointed, perhaps even ruined. How many women had Cecil caused to cry? What did he do when their tears fell, when he told them he would never marry them?

At least Abigail would be spared that insult.

Tedric fingered the embroidered kerchief. He hoped and prayed that Abigail had given the gifts to him as a gesture of appreciation for his kindness as her future brother-in-law. He hoped and prayed she hadn't made the mistake of falling in love with him. If she had, no good could come of it. He was miserable enough, knowing he could never have her. His desire was for her never to experience such regret and shame.

Cecil stirred with a groan. "Huh? Where, where am I? Lizzie, where are you?"

The unpleasant image of such a hardened woman seared into Tedric's dreams of lovely Abigail. "Lizzie is in London," he snapped.

"London?" Cecil rolled over. He looked at Tedric and blinked. "Then where am I?"

"You are in our coach. We shall be home shortly."

"My head." Cecil placed his palm on his forehead. "Have you a nip of ale with you? Nothing cures a headache like a snout full."

"No." Tedric deliberately kept all traces of compassion out of his voice.

"I might have known you would not be able to offer any liquid refreshment. You always were a prig, attending church services every week and refusing to drink up with the rest of us."

Tedric knew that nothing could be gained by taking the bait of his brother's insult. "Rest is what you need," Tedric answered. "You will have time for a short nap before you are due at the Pettigrews'. I am sure a few winks in your own bed will prove much more refreshing than trying to sleep here."

"The Pettigrews'?" Cecil's eyes flashed. "Oh. I remember. I am supposed to meet them tonight, am I not?" His tone indicated that he hoped Tedric would tell him he was mistaken.

"Yes. You are due there after dinner."

"After dinner?" Cecil lifted his overweight frame on one arm, then pushed himself upright. He placed a hand on his stomach. "Why, my brother, could you not have secured us a bit of free prog? I suppose we'll have to scrounge together something for ourselves from the kitchen." A mischievous smile touched his lips.

"I am glad to see your sense of humor is returning." Tedric paused. "I arranged for the meeting to take place after dinner because I was not sure I would be able to secure your arrival any earlier. Not to mention, I imagine the Pettigrews would expect much better table manners from their guests than the women do in the houses where you usually dine."

Cecil chuckled, though not good-naturedly. "Indeed, my brother. I am glad to see that your sense of humor is returning."

"Very well. Now that we are all in a fine humor, you should be anticipating a splendid evening in the company of your lovely betrothed and your future father-in-law."

Cecil's mouth pursed into an unhappy line. "A stifling evening in the company of prudish nobs, no doubt."

"You leap to judgments without evidence."

"Oh? And what do you know about the Pettigrews?"

"More than you do," Tedric argued. "Abigail is quite lovely and charming."

"Is she? According to Henry Hanover, she is plain and shy."

"She is neither plain nor shy," Tedric countered.

"Spoken like a faithful brother-in-law." He leaned closer and looked Tedric in the eye. "Or is it more like a smitten lover?"

Unwelcome guilt pierced Tedric. Did the light in his eyes betray him? He managed to compose himself well enough to answer. "She is a young woman of breeding and refinement, and if you would remember your own breeding, you would neither insult me nor listen to the likes of Henry Hanover."

"Surely my friend Henry has as much good breeding as Miss Pettigrew. That will be aptly demonstrated by her willingness to marry me, regardless of your feelings for her." Cecil didn't wait for Tedric's reply. "You say she is so delightful. I doubt it. The women of breeding and refinement with whom I have become acquainted are barely tolerable. I do not wish to spend any more time with Abigail's sort than is absolutely necessary, thank you." Cecil folded his arms.

"Is she truly that disgusting to you?"

Cecil raised his shoulders and palms in a gesture of dismissal. "I am sure that, like all women, she is not without her charms. But that is not the point. I do not wish to be near her, or any Pettigrew, for that matter."

"You will never secure an heir that way."

"When duty to God and country beckons, I will answer."

Tedric hoped that Cecil didn't see him shudder. The thought of his brother touching innocent Abigail. . .

"But I am not certain I will answer that call with Abigail Pettigrew."

"What do you mean to say?"

Cecil leaned toward Tedric. "I am saying that there is more to the situation than you know." He leaned back. "That is all I am at liberty to say."

"I do not know what you are trying to imply, but I will have you to know, Abigail Pettigrew is a lady in the truest sense of the word."

"Oh, my, but you have become enchanted by her feminine wiles. I can see this will be more difficult than I thought. Perhaps I can put off the appointment." Cecil placed his palm on his forehead once more. "I do believe I am feeling odd."

"No doubt. However, you do not have my sympathies as you have no one to blame but yourself for your ailments," Tedric pointed out. "I will not make any excuses for you. You must keep your appointment with her father. He is expecting you."

"You cannot force me to go. I shall send a messenger—"

"You shall do no such thing. You will prepare to meet them. And to be sure you do, I shall drive you there myself."

Cecil glowered, but Tedric met his stare without flinching. Defeated, Cecil laid his head back on the seat and fell asleep once again.

With at least another hour remaining in their journey, Tedric contemplated his plight. If only he could change places with Cecil! If only he, not his brother, were due at the Pettigrew estate that evening!

But it was not to be.

Though Tedric didn't like to think of himself as vain, he often caught women noticing him. If bold, they batted their eyelashes. If shy, they looked away when they realized he saw them. Despite the many opportunities that had presented themselves since he first became aware of the fairer sex, Tedric had never been taken with anyone as he had with Abigail. From the first moment he saw her clutching her diary, an angry look covering her beautiful face, he had loved her.

He felt a smile tickle his lips when he recalled his first words to her. "My, but are we not peppery on this fine evening!"

The words, such a fine description of Abigail in her state of vexation, had annoyed her beyond description. He held back a chuckle.

His jaw tightened when he recalled the second time he'd seen Abigail. She had transformed from a fireball to a pale figure, collapsed from cold, fright, and perhaps not a small bit of humiliation. He was glad. Yes, glad that Henry Hanover hadn't met her. If he had. . .

Tedric didn't want to think about it. He preferred to dwell on Abigail's stay with him at the estate. Sometimes, when he watched her go about her duties, he could almost pretend. . .

No! His fantasies were wrong. Wrong. He could never have Abigail. Not now, not ever.

Tedric had already slipped by defending Abigail too

strongly during his conversation with Cecil. That would never happen again. He would control his tongue with all the willpower he possessed. If anyone uttered a word against Abigail, Cecil would have to defend her honor. That would be his duty as her husband, after all.

Not only would Tedric remain mute, he would play the role of dutiful brother to Cecil and future brother-in-law to Abigail for the next few months. He would do anything and everything in his power to ensure the success of their wedding. He would host prenuptial parties and even help Cecil with honeymoon arrangements. His performance would be flawless.

No one would ever know. No one would ever suspect that he loved her.

A silent petition popped into his mind. *Father in heaven, forgive me. I am already on the brink of sin. Do not allow me to covet my brother's wife. I beg of You, save me from myself.*

So intense was Tedric's prayer that he uttered the last thought aloud, disturbing his sleeping brother.

"Huh? What was that?" Cecil murmured.

"Nothing. Just a morning prayer."

There. At least he wasn't a liar too.

Tedric looked out the small window. Only a few more miles, and they would be home. Home. After the wedding, he wouldn't be able to call the estate "home." The day after the nuptials, Tedric would leave for London. Perhaps he would buy a town house there. Perhaps when a beautiful woman looked his way, he would return the favor.

He could only hope and pray. Pray that the miles between him and Abigail would be enough to make him forget.

fifteen

The night had come! The night Abigail was to see Tedric once more. The night that he would arrive to set the date of the wedding!

Griselda's admonitions about Tedric's adventures in London had upset her, but Abigail yearned for Tedric all the same. How she longed to see him again, to hear his voice, to be close enough to breathe his masculine scent. That very evening, it would happen. She would be in his presence once more!

"Why am I so eager?" she muttered. "He does not love me."

"Father in heaven," she prayed, "why did You choose to place me in a marriage of unrequited love? How can I escape such a fate?

The answer came swiftly.

You do not need to escape.

A knock on the door interrupted her petition. Surely her visitor was Missy. "Come in."

The maid entered and dropped a curtsy. "Are ye ready for me to dress yer hair, M'lady?"

Abigail nodded.

"I'll be curlin' it special tonight." Missy's bouncing movements betrayed her excitement.

"Are you happy for me or at the prospect of leaving here soon?" Abigail couldn't resist asking.

"I'm happy fer ye." Missy paused. "And I look forward to leavin' here, I do. The weddin' will take place soon, I'm hopin'."

"When my new brother or sister is a half year old."

"That long, eh?"

"I shall need time to plan."

"I know yer weddin' day will be the talk of the parish. Not to mention all yer prenuptial celebrations."

"Quite a different story from the first time I tried to marry," Abigail quipped.

"Well, everyone who knows yer family is expectin' a big show." Missy perfected a ringlet and viewed Abigail's reflection in the mirror. "Ye'll make the most beautiful bride I've ever seen, ye will."

"Thank you, although I do not believe a word of your flattery."

"What dress will ye be wearin' tonight?"

"Your favorite. The rose-colored one."

"The one with the darin' neckline? My, but ye must be wantin' to impress him."

Abigail saw herself blush in the mirror. "I have some lace that will fill the neckline in nicely."

"'Tis a pity, that is."

"Missy, you are quite naughty." Abigail couldn't stifle a giggle.

An hour passed as Missy and Abigail readied her to see her beloved. Satisfied that she looked her best and that enough pleasant lavender toilette water wafted from her skin, Abigail dismissed her maid.

For a moment, she almost wished she hadn't. When would Tedric arrive? If only Missy were still with her. They could talk about the weather, the garden, anything. She would be willing to broach any subject to pass the time.

Abigail realized that idle chitchat was not what the Lord wanted. Rather, she felt led to meditate upon His plans for her.

But to what end? No matter how much she prayed, Abigail failed to understand why the Lord willed her to have a husband who didn't love her. She knew she wasn't the only member of the aristocracy to marry for reasons other than love. Her father's concern was to combine the two families' lineage and fortunes. Her happiness was secondary, and she knew it. Yet happiness was just within her grasp. If only Tedric could love her!

If the Lord has willed me to spend the rest of my life serving a man who doesn't love me, I—

Abigail shuddered. She could never follow Griselda's unthinkable suggestion that she take a lover. Besides, if marital duties were so hideous, why would any woman seek out yet another man? None of Griselda's hints or advice made any sense to Abigail. Her conscience, satisfied that she would keep God's commandments, asked her another question: *So what will you do?*

I will love him and show him my love nevertheless. Maybe then he will come to love me. Maybe even with as much fervor as I love him!

How do I begin, Lord?

As always when she contemplated the solution to a dilemma, Abigail looked to her Bible. She knew many of the verses about love, but decided to turn to one of the most well known passages, the thirteenth chapter of 1 Corinthians: "Charity suffereth long, and is kind; charity envieth not; charity vaunteth not itself, is not puffed up, Doth not behave itself unseemly, seeketh not her own, is not easily provoked, thinketh no evil."

How could she be so generous with Tedric, a man who sought comfort in gaming halls and, even worse, in the arms of other women?

The hinges of her bedchamber door creaked. Abigail jumped and clutched her hand to her chest at once.

"Did I frighten you?"

She turned to her visitor. "Griselda! Yes, you did." Since Abigail and her stepmother had become closer, Abigail had been permitted to call her stepmother by her Christian name.

"I beg your pardon. I did not realize you were in deep contemplation." She observed Abigail's frock. "I see you are wearing one of my favorite old dresses."

Abigail nodded.

"It looks well on you. I confess, I was feeling a bit guilty about not having a new gown made for you to wear upon this occasion. Yet now that I see how my dress compliments you,

I believe you could not have worn better."

"Thank you."

Griselda's attention turned to the open Bible. "Consulting Scripture, I see. Are you anxious?"

"Would you not be if you were in my position?"

Griselda nodded. "That is why I came here to see you." She waddled to the side of Abigail's bed and patted the space on the high bed where Abigail sat. "May I?"

Abigail nodded. "Unless the vanity chair is more comfortable."

Griselda studied the seat. "Perhaps that might be more prudent, given I would have to climb onto your bed," she answered with an oblique reference to her advanced state of expectancy.

"Why did you want to see me now?" Abigail asked as she watched Griselda situate herself in the chair.

"I wanted to see if you were feeling better about your impending marriage since we last talked."

"Does it matter? I shall be married whether I like it or not."

"I know this must be hard for you, Abigail. I always knew you were the idealistic one, but I never realized how blind you were to the facts of arranged marriages. If you had been born to parents of another class, you might enjoy the luxury of marrying for love. After all, what does a scullery maid care about money? Her chances of marrying an heir to a fortune or even a title are nonexistent." Griselda leaned toward her. "You would not really want that for yourself, would you?"

Abigail thought about Missy. "At least Missy's beau sees her every day."

Griselda leaned back. "Do you mean that stable boy at the Suttons'? What did you say his name is. . .Jack?"

"Yes. He is the one she loves. And I cannot say that I blame her. He cuts quite a fine figure, and she says she loves to run her fingers through his red curls." Abigail felt herself blush, no doubt as red as Jack's locks. She should have never betrayed what Missy had shared in confidence. "Please do not mention that I let slip what she told me."

"As if I had not already heard her talking to Mattie about her illicit union."

"Illicit union? Why," Abigail huffed, "Missy would never do such a thing!"

"That is not your concern, unless she should become in a family way."

"Griselda! How could you suggest such a thing?"

"Never mind that." Griselda patted Abigail's hand. "The fact of the matter is, what does any stable boy have to offer a woman? A lifetime of toil and the smell of manure hanging about him, that is what." Griselda shrugged. "Not that she, as a member of her class, can do better."

"But if he loves her. . ."

"I suppose he could love you too, if he thought he could get his hands on a fortune and ensure that his children are heirs to titles."

"What are you saying?" Abigail asked.

"I am saying love means very little within good marriages."

"Do you mean that you do not love my father or that you have a bad marriage?"

"I have grown quite fond of your father over the years we have been married."

"Only quite fond? Is that all the emotion you can muster?" Abigail shook her head. "How sad for Father."

"How sad for me." Griselda, usually direct, looked down at her knees. "I can never compete with your mother or even with you."

"Griselda! You never compete with me. And Mother is with the Lord in heaven. She would not wish for you and Father to have an unhappy union." How Abigail managed to express such comfort toward her difficult stepmother, she would never know. Perhaps the Lord was working in her already.

"Thank you," Griselda whispered.

At that moment, Abigail understood more about her stepmother than she ever had. All the insults, all the harsh words had been spoken out of insecurity.

"And I am certain," Griselda was saying, "that you will grow fond of Lord Sutton as time passes. Wait and see."

"But I don't want to be fond of my husband. I want to love him with all my heart. He should be second only to God."

"You either have your head in the clouds or in the Bible too much, my dear."

"Really? Must life be this way, Griselda?" Abigail felt unwanted tears threaten.

"Maybe not." Griselda let out an audible sigh. "I can see that you feel your situation is quite hopeless. I know I should not make such an offer, but I will." She paused. "Do you want me to speak to your father, Abigail? Perhaps he can find another eligible bachelor." Griselda's eyebrows rose in sudden delight. "Someone with an even larger fortune?"

Abigail knew that Griselda meant well in her sympathy, but her tongue displayed all too well her greed.

"Thank you, but no." She paused. "And thank you for talking to me. Your words have given me the resolve I need."

"Resolve? To do what? To demand that the wedding be called off?" Griselda's eyes took on a light of fear.

"No. The resolve to live my life as God sees fit, no matter what that may mean."

A knock on the door interrupted.

"Yes?" Abigail called.

Missy entered and curtsied. "Your betrothed has arrived, M'lady. Your father requests yer presence in the parlor."

"Thank you." Abigail's heart suddenly felt as though it would beat its way through the rose-colored gown. She sent Griselda an imploring look. "Will you come with me?"

"I am afraid not." Griselda nodded toward her belly, indicating that she should not enter the presence of a stranger in her condition.

"I beg pardon," Abigail apologized. "My mind is elsewhere."

"You are understandably nervous."

Griselda extended her hand. Abigail accepted the gesture and allowed her stepmother to give her hand a small squeeze.

"All will be well," Griselda assured her. "I just know it."

Abigail sent her a weak smile. "Will you pray with me?"

Griselda nodded. "Would you like for me to say the prayer?"

"Would you?"

Griselda bowed her head, and Abigail followed suit.

"Father in Heaven," Griselda petitioned, "be with Abigail as she meets with her betrothed. Bless them as they plan their wedding. Be with them always in their life together. We ask for Your will, amen."

"Thank you." Abigail did what would have been unthinkable only a month before. She leaned over and embraced Griselda. When they broke their hold on each other, Abigail felt a teardrop in her eye.

"Now, now. Do not cry. You do not want Lord Sutton to see you with your face all red and puffed, do you?"

Abigail shook her head and grabbed the kerchief lying on top of her dresser. After wiping her eyes, she looked in the mirror and decided she looked well enough to see Tedric again. All the same, she looked to Griselda for final approval.

"You look well now." Griselda's smile was bittersweet. "Good luck."

Feeling as though she needed much more than luck, Abigail was not so cheerful as she descended the stairs. Her nerves were in such a state that she felt as though her entire body would shake enough to invite comment.

If only he had written, maybe I wouldn't feel so insecure, so vexed, and so weak-kneed.

Helpless to remedy the past, Abigail had no choice. She stepped through the foyer and headed for the parlor to her future, the one that would begin that night.

Abigail tarried in the entrance. Her gaze fell to the fire, the center of any room on a chilly night in early spring. Her father stood in front of the fireplace, talking with a gentleman she did not know. The man looked as though he might have been handsome a decade ago, but his hair was thinning and he sported a paunch that suggested he had consumed too much rich food and had adventured through a high life over the years. Noting pasty skin, she wondered if he ever submitted himself to the out of doors.

After considering his appearance, she mulled over the possible identities of this man in her mind. Abigail could only conclude that he was Tedric's London solicitor.

At that moment, he threw back his head and laughed with enough uproar to fill the room. Father joined in whatever amusement they shared, though his response was a refined chuckle. Abigail noted the glass of wine in the stranger's hand. Perhaps intoxication caused every joke to be more amusing to the solicitor than when he was sober.

Abigail held back a grimace. Where was Tedric? She scanned the room and spotted him alone in a far corner. His fingers held a small statue of Venus that her parents had purchased on their long-ago honeymoon. Her heart felt as though it jumped into her throat and fell back to her stomach. Was Tedric just as anxious as she? Perhaps that explained why he sequestered himself away from the other men.

"There you are, Abigail!" Father motioned for her to come to his side.

She nodded to her father and then set her gaze upon Tedric. Tedric! She never thought it possible that he could look more charming and handsome in person than in her imagination, but he had managed to achieve the feat.

Abigail eyed him in a way that she knew expressed her naked emotions. She watched for the look of love she longed for and anticipated in return.

"How do you do, Miss Pettigrew?"

"How do you do," Abigail managed to sputter.

She watched as Tedric bowed his head toward the statue in his hands and continued to study it as though he were assigned to memorize its every detail.

Abigail composed her mouth into a straight line and kept her eyes unblinking. Surely Father would not object to her betrothed greeting her with a bit less formality. So why didn't he? What game was Tedric playing? Why did he torture her so? "Where is the butler?" Father wondered aloud. "He should have returned with the wine by now."

"He is certainly slow about it." Emphasizing his point, the strange man reached for the open bottle on the sidebar and poured the remainder of its contents into his empty glass.

"Never mind. I am certain he will be returning shortly." Father smiled at her. "Abigail, you are here now and I can make the introductions."

Abigail sent her gaze to Tedric's corner and waited for him to step forward while Father introduced the solicitor, but he did not. Reticence seemed to have struck Tedric cold. Perhaps he would relax once they had dispensed with formalities.

Hopeful, she returned her attention to Father. His eyes gleamed with the pride she often saw in his face. Did she see a touch of mist as well?

He looked at the man standing beside him. "Sutton, this is my daughter, Abigail Pettigrew."

The man responded by looking her up and down. Unmistakable lust filled his expression. At that moment she regretted wearing the rose-colored dress, despite the modest lace that covered her throat.

"How do you do?" she managed to utter.

"Abigail," Father said, "this is your betrothed. Lord Cecil Sutton."

sixteen

"What?" Abigail blurted. "This cannot be!"

"Indeed he is," Father said.

Abigail swallowed and stared at the man standing before her. Surely this loud, boorish, pursy man could not be her intended. Not when she loved Tedric with every fiber of her being!

Tedric! She sent her gaze to the corner where her beloved stood, realizing even as she did that her eyes were wide with pleading. He watched the scene with the intensity of one witnessing the climax of an opera. Why didn't he say something?

"Abigail! Where are your manners?" Father asked. He turned to Cecil. "I beg your pardon. My daughter is obviously quite taken by your presence. She is justifiably nervous about seeing you."

"That is quite understandable." He tilted his head up with an attitude of superiority.

So Lord Sutton was vain too!

"I can forgive your reaction, Miss Pettigrew." Cecil looked down his nose as much as was possible considering its round appearance.

"But—" Abigail protested.

"Please, Abigail!" Father corrected. "Greet your betrothed properly."

"My betrothed? But I told you, he is not my betrothed!" Abigail cut her glance to Tedric. His mouth had formed an O. He stood in place, clutching the statue as though it were the anchor of a sinking ship that he captained. She wanted to run over to him, to shake him out of his stupor. With all her might, she subdued the impulse. The stricken look on his face stopped her. As always, Tedric was a gentleman. In a moment of epiphany, she realized that in his meekness, Tedric displayed more heroism than if he had challenged Cecil to a duel.

"What is the matter with you, Abigail? Of course Lord Sutton is your betrothed. We have spoken of nothing else for the past several months." Though hardly ever ruffled, at that moment, Father had become flustered. He appealed to Cecil. "Again, I beg your pardon, Lord Sutton."

Cecil took a swig of his drink. "I had no idea your daughter possessed such an excitable nature."

"She is not in the habit of displaying such emotion," Father apologized. "I am certain that once Abigail has overcome the awe she must feel from being in your presence, she will prove to be a most agreeable wife."

"I shall be an agreeable wife to the man who will be my husband, naturally. But this is not the man I know as my betrothed," Abigail protested.

"The man you know?" Father asked.

"You already know a man?" The sly smile on Cecil's face portrayed his obvious intimation.

"Whatever do you mean?" Abigail asked.

"Of course not, Lord Sutton. I assure you—" Father implored.

"Tedric," Abigail turned her face to the man she loved. "Tedric, do something!"

"What would you have him do?" Cecil asked before Tedric could answer.

Abigail huffed. "I would have him tell you both that he is my betrothed. That is what I would have him do."

"Indeed?" Cecil's expression became blank and then he let out a hearty gale of laughter. "You think my baby brother is your intended?"

Abigail gasped. No, it could not be! Tedric couldn't be the younger brother! He had to be Lord Sutton.

"Baby brother? Tedric is hardly a baby." She narrowed her eyes at Cecil. "And I don't believe he is your brother!" Abigail shook so much that controlling her voice was a difficult feat. "How can you be the brother to a man such as Tedric?"

Cecil chuckled. "If you mean the man standing in the corner, yes, that is my younger brother." Cecil turned to Tedric. "Perhaps there is another side to this story?"

"But of course." Tedric nodded and returned the statue of Venus to its place before striding toward them with the confidence Abigail had grown to know and love.

"This woman says that you are her betrothed. Do you care to explain?" Cecil tilted the glass to his lips.

"I know nothing about which she speaks. I assure you, this is a misunderstanding."

"But—" Abigail wasn't sure whether to scream or to cry. "Tedric, how could you?"

"If you will not explain, then perhaps Miss Pettigrew can enlighten us," Cecil said.

"Yes, Abigail," Father agreed.

Abigail looked at Cecil. "I–I—"

"Are you saying that my brother has led you to believe that you were betrothed to him?" Cecil prompted.

Abigail tried to think. "He never said as much, but. . ."

"But what?" Father's voice was harsh.

Cecil set his glass down on an end table and folded his arms. "Yes. I am interested in learning about your stay with him too."

"If you are accusing your brother of acting dishonorably, you are mistaken," Abigail said. "Nothing could be further from the truth. He was nothing less than a gentleman the entire time I remained at the estate," she informed the men. "He helped me to learn how to be a good wife and to be mistress of the manor."

Cecil shot a look at Father. "I should think your wife would have seen to her training in managing a large household."

"My wife performed her duties superbly, and she taught Abigail to do the same," Father protested. "I have no notion as to why my daughter gives such tribute to your brother."

Cecil rubbed his chin with his thumb and forefinger and turned to Tedric. "Indeed. Have you anything to say for yourself?"

"I can say merely this: During Miss Pettigrew's stay at the estate, I acted the perfect gentleman, and she was always the lady."

"We only walked in the garden," Abigail admitted before thinking.

"What?" Father's voice rose with disapproval. "You allowed this man to take you for a walk, unescorted by a chaperone?" He swept his hand toward Tedric. "And you." He eyed Tedric with the hatred of a sworn enemy. "You took advantage of her innocence?"

"Never!" Tedric cried.

"Never for a moment!" Abigail agreed. "We barely walked fifty paces down the garden path. Any one of the servants could have come upon us without a moment's notice."

"She speaks the truth," Tedric agreed. "I implore you to interview them if there is any doubt."

Abigail took her father's hands in hers. "Father, I am the one who asked Tedric to walk with me, just for a few moments, long enough for me to give him a small gift."

"You gave him gifts?" Cecil's tone betrayed his suspicion.

"But I thought, I thought—" Abigail balled a piece of the fabric of her dress in her hand. She sent Tedric a look of appeal. "I thought you were my betrothed."

"I still do not understand how this could have happened," Father said. "I was certain you knew, Abigail, that you were betrothed to Lord Sutton, not his younger brother."

"How was I to know Lord Sutton had a younger brother?" Abigail asked. "How was I to know he had a brother at all? Lord Sutton was never present at the estate. I just assumed. . ."

"She is right," Cecil admitted. "Had I been at the estate instead of in London and had I taken the least bit of interest in the woman who was to become my bride, Miss Pettigrew would have known without a doubt that I was her betrothed. Instead, I let my brother take the place I should have occupied in her heart and mind."

"Without intention, I promise you," Tedric said. "I had no

idea that Miss Pettigrew thought for a moment that she and I were engaged to be married. This development comes as as much of a shock to me as it does to you."

"Does it?" Cecil's lips curved into an unconvinced bow. "What did you think when you accepted gifts from my betrothed?"

Tedric looked him in the eye. "I believed she was being the lovely young woman that she is—an agreeable future sister-in-law. I thought she was giving me tokens to show her appreciation for my kindness. After all, she had been abandoned at the estate by her parents."

"Much to my regret." Father swallowed, a certain sign that he felt as much remorse as Tedric ever could. He appealed to Cecil. "The night Abigail made the shameful error of attempting to elope with Lord Hanover, your brother rescued her from certain death, as you well know. He did bring Abigail here first, but my wife turned him away without consulting me. He understandably took her to your estate. Where else could he go with her?"

"Indeed." Cecil nodded.

"Had I been awake," Father said, "and had I been told about the turn of events, I would have insisted my daughter stay here. She never would have been compromised or could have been in a position to compromise your brother. I extend my deepest apologies for the poor judgment of my wife and the consequences of her decision."

"Consequences. Yes," Cecil said. "When we spoke earlier today, I suspected Tedric had become, shall we say, smitten with your daughter."

Abigail watched Tedric. His lips tightened and a light of guilt entered his eyes. So he did love her too!

Cecil eyed Abigail. "Do you return my younger brother's affections, Miss Pettigrew?"

Abigail wanted to blurt a resounding yes, but Father's voice stopped her.

"Of course not, Sutton. Do not be ridiculous."

Cecil ignored Father and looked Abigail in the eye. "Think

carefully before you respond, Miss Pettigrew. A match made with me would be much more profitable to you and your family than a union with my brother. Remember, he stands to inherit none of the Sutton land holdings." Cecil sneered, "Is that not true, Tedric?"

"That is true. My wealth does not, nor will it ever, compare to my brother's." Tedric winced with each word as though he were being pricked with daggers.

"Is money all you care about?" Abigail asked. "Father, you taught me to know better! Did not our Lord and Savior tell the rich young ruler to give up everything he had to follow Him?"

"Mr. Sutton is not your Lord and Savior."

"No, but he follows my Lord and Savior." Abigail felt her jaw tighten as she looked at Cecil. "Unlike you, Sir."

"Please," Father begged Cecil. "Pay no attention to the ravings of a young girl. Allow me to explain everything." He turned to Tedric. "If you would be so kind as to excuse us."

Tedric hesitated long enough to cast a glance at Abigail before he agreed. "I shall be waiting in the carriage, Cecil."

Abigail watched him depart. She wanted with all her heart to follow him. "May I be excused as well?"

"No. Not until he has situated himself in the carriage." Father drew the curtain back and observed as Tedric made his way across the front lawn and to the waiting coach.

"Now Abigail." He nodded. "You may be excused. Do not think you can go after him. I shall be watching through the window."

Abigail could see from the stern looks on the men's faces that debate was useless. "Yes, Father. I bid you a good evening, Lord Sutton." She nodded and curtsied, then fled to the hallway.

So Tedric is not a known gambler and rake after all, but the godly man I have come to know. . .and love!

But her love could not overcome the inevitable. She was betrothed to Cecil, not Tedric. She could never be Tedric's wife. Unwanted tears filled her eyes. Powerless to resist temptation, she hovered just outside the doorway. She had to listen.

"Once again, I beg your forgiveness, Lord Sutton," Father said. "Despite my daughter's words, I do not think for a moment that she has become infatuated with your brother. And if she believes she has, I am certain she is misinterpreting your brother's kindness for romantic love. You see, she is quite sheltered and innocent. A young girl's head is easily turned."

"I already know how easily her head is turned," Cecil answered. "Henry Hanover and I frequent the same London establishments. He told me about how she attempted to elope with him."

Although she couldn't see her father's face, she could feel his embarrassment. Shame gripped her.

"That was all a misunderstanding," Father said. "I hope that we can put whatever errors might have happened in the past aside and forget them forever. And as for your brother—"

"It is not the past that concerns me, but the present," Cecil answered. "And it is not your daughter's behavior that I find unforgivable, but yours."

"Mine?"

"Yes." Cecil paused. "I recently received word from my solicitor that your resources are not all that you first indicated to me."

She could almost hear Father's mind working to find a suitable answer. "Our situation has grown worse since the betrothal."

"Indeed? Are you saying that you cannot provide the dowry you promised?"

"I will try—"

"You will succeed if you want this wedding to take place."

"I beg your pardon, but how dare you question my integrity! I know not of what so-called deception you speak. When I entered into the contract with you, I had the resources available for the dowry." Father's voice betrayed his indignation. "Why, in my younger years, a lesser insult would have constituted a challenge to duel."

"I have no intention of challenging you to a duel. Even if that were my intent, you would be wise not to act hastily since we would be outside of the law and because your wife will soon deliver of a child." Cecil's voice turned soft. "I beg pardon, but if you were to be questioned in a court of law, you would be found guilty of deception, and that you know quite well."

"I must say, Lord Sutton, I never intended to deceive you in any way. I have always been straightforward about my wealth," Father elaborated. "As for Abigail, I confess, she acted impetuously in regard to Henry Hanover." He sighed. "I am not proud of her conduct."

Father's words made Abigail blush hot. Mortified, she slid against the wall and sank to the floor.

"Since you are well acquainted with Lord Hanover, you know firsthand how he can charm the ladies," Father continued.

"According to his recollection, he gave your daughter no encouragement," Cecil reminded him.

"Perhaps not to his eyes, but your friend is accustomed to the flirtations of sophisticates, women with the experience to discern a man's true intentions underneath a facade of frivolous conversation. My daughter is neither sophisticated nor flirtatious," Father said. "In fact, she spends most of her leisure in solitude, writing in her diary, much to the annoyance of her stepmother." Father chuckled. "I can promise you that Abigail has been sheltered from the world all of her life. There is no doubt in my mind that even Lord Hanover will tell you that she remains unsullied."

"I am aware of your daughter's unblemished past, which is the reason I agreed to the betrothal when you first approached me. As for Henry, he has already given me his assurances, and since we are lifelong friends, I trust his word," Cecil answered.

Abigail breathed a sigh of relief in spite of herself. Although she had thought little of her reputation when she tried to chase Henry to the altar, since meeting Tedric, she had come to treasure her purity.

"I admit, I am not so sure about my brother. I do not blame Miss Pettigrew for her reported behavior since she indeed thought Tedric was her betrothed. But I see a light in his eyes that matches hers."

"As do I," Father admitted.

Though Abigail could hear the unhappiness in his voice, she clasped her hands and brought them up to her chest, right where she could feel her beating heart. So even Cecil and her father could see the love in Tedric's eyes. His love wasn't the product of her imagination!

"I am sure her childish romantic ideas will pass as soon as you are married. I hope you will not hold her impetuousness against her." Father's words filled Abigail with distress.

"I repeat, my quarrel is not with your daughter."

Cecil's answer would have pleased any other woman, but not Abigail. She didn't want Cecil to forgive her.

Lord in heaven, please lead Lord Sutton to dissolve our contract. Please.

As soon as her silent petition ended, Abigail wondered if she were wrong to pray it. Yet the plea was from the deepest recesses of her heart. Would the Lord see fit to let her live with the love of her life?

"Though your daughter is far from a ravishing London beauty," Cecil continued, "her appearance is pleasant enough. Her voice, when not raised in vexation, is pleasing to the ears."

"In that event, you should be eager to wed my daughter," said Father.

Abigail groaned inwardly.

"I should be," Cecil said, "except that your deception has been your downfall. When you betrothed me to Abigail, you led me to believe that you were still quite wealthy. My understanding was that your fortune had not been diminished in the least since your family has held this estate."

"That is correct. I hold the same number of acres—more, even—than my ancestors, including my own father. Abigail's mother brought with her a not inconsiderable dowry to my irst marriage, including additional lands." Pride rang through is voice. "You can be confident that not one parcel of Pettigrew land has ever been sold for any reason."

"But your fortune. It has dwindled down to nothing."

Father hesitated. " 'Nothing' is too strong a word. I admit, ny financial situation is not what it once was." She heard Father set down his own glass with a soft thud. "I thought hat was common knowledge."

His voice had softened to a whisper. Abigail imagined him asting his eyes downward. She winced.

Cecil's voice bespoke his arrogance. "I knew from reliable ources that your finances were leaner than in the past, but only recently did my London solicitor bring to my attention he extent of your plight."

"Unfortunately, I was swindled when I made what I thought were prudent business investments." Father let out a sigh. "My bank accounts have not yet fully recovered. I am certain they will in due course, at which time I can make good on the contract."

"And after that, you are hoping the Sutton union can better your situation?"

"Is that so unreasonable?"

"Perhaps not. But you should have been honest with me from the start. Why did you not tell me about your finances?" Cecil asked.

Abigail wanted to spit in Cecil's face. Why should her father be honest with someone such as Cecil? A cad and rake didn't deserve to be treated with honesty and respect.

"I thought you realized that we are not as wealthy as you are," Father answered. "A simple look around the estate shows one that much. Why, we do not employ half the staff that you do, even though our household is larger. Perhaps, if over the course of the past few months, you had enjoyed our hospitality more often. . ."

"I see your point. Nevertheless, I shall not marry your daughter. Please make my excuses, and make certain she knows that my decision has nothing to do with her person."

Cecil's dismissal of her brought Abigail to her feet. She burst into the parlor.

"Why do you not tell me yourself, Lord Sutton?" Abigail breathed her contempt into his name. "Are you such a coward that you are afraid to face me?"

"Abigail!" Father corrected.

Cecil posed his own question. "Who would wish to face a young woman with the poor manners to eavesdrop on a private conversation?"

The butler chose to enter at that moment. "I beg forgiveness, but I had difficulty locating the particular vintage of red wine that Lord Sutton requested."

Father raised his hand. "That is quite all right. Do not uncork the bottle. There will be no celebration here tonight."

The butler's eyes widened. "Yes, Sir." He bowed and exited as quickly as he had entered.

"Now where were we?" Father folded his arms and glowered at Cecil. "Oh, yes. You were accusing my daughter of displaying ill manners."

"Indeed. I should say that tonight's events have been a blessing," Cecil observed. "It has come to my attention that to wed your daughter would be a mistake. Not only has she shown herself disagreeable, but the Pettigrew name has been diminished in my eyes."

"Regrettable indeed, but not so with our friends," Father pointed out. "So your decision is final, then. You are breaking off the betrothal." His voice was flat.

"Yes."

"In that case, perhaps I should consider taking you to court for breach of contract," Father suggested.

"If you believe you can induce me to pay you to forget this unfortunate incident, you are sadly mistaken. Your case, particularly once my solicitor produces your financial records for review, would never hold forth in a court of law."

"I ask that you honor your contract. Not for myself, but for

Abigail's honor."

Cecil glanced at Abigail. "Anyone who witnessed such a display as your daughter's would hardly be eager to wed her."

Abigail had no desire to apologize to such a vile man, but she knew for the sake of her family name, she must. She curtsied. "I beg your indulgence, Lord Sutton. I have been taught better than to eavesdrop. Forgive me for succumbing to the temptation."

Cecil's gaze rested upon her figure. Abigail tried not to squirm.

"Perhaps I was hasty in questioning your manners." The shadow of a smile touched Cecil's face. "You can be forgiven, considering the import of the discussion. I am sorry you had to bother your pretty head with the dry details of financial affairs."

"Please know that my father is a man of honor, a gentleman in every way that counts."

"Loyalty. I like that in a woman." His scrutiny visited Abigail's figure yet again. "Perhaps we could arrange—"

"No," Father said.

"No?" Cecil lifted his nose and bored his stare into Father's face. "Emotions have run high here tonight. Perhaps if I return tomorrow. . ."

"No. I shall allow Abigail to remain a spinster and reduce my household staff to a cook and a maid-of-all-work before I allow her to wed you."

"Father!" Abigail nearly jumped for joy. "Do you mean that?"

"Yes, Abigail. You do not have to marry this man."

"Oh, Father!" Abigail threw her arms around his neck. "Thank you!"

Cecil cleared his throat. "Though you are quick to discard me, certainly you realize that gentlemen of my rank and position are sought after by many women."

At St. Giles, no doubt, Abigail wanted to burst out.

She held her tongue. The shady section of London was

only whispered about behind closed doors of polite society. Never would Abigail reveal to Cecil or to her father that she was cognizant of such a place.

"Lady Olivia Hamilton has indicated that she does not find me so repulsive." He stared at them both. "You do know of her, do you not? The London heiress?"

"Yes, I am aware of her and her vast fortune. And her reputation." Father's last statement intimated that he was sending Cecil a veiled message.

"Your opinion of Lady Hamilton matters not to me. She is a lady of fine family and breeding. Should she agree to a betrothal, ours will be a powerful match." He sniffed. "Do not bother yourself. I shall see myself to the door. Good evening."

As soon as he left, Abigail hugged Father once more.

"Now, now. There is no need for such spectacle."

Abigail broke the embrace. "I just want you to know how grateful I am to you."

"I had no idea you found Lord Sutton so revolting," Father said. "I know the peak of his comeliness has passed and that he likes to have his pleasures, but I was told he is quite appealing to the opposite sex." He shook his head. "That only goes to show how wrong gossip can be."

"Is it? He seems to think himself irresistible."

Father took Abigail's hands in his. "I am sorry for making such a match for you, Abigail. I wanted you to be well situated. The Sutton name and the fact that Cecil is the eldest son and stands to inherit such a great deal of land—"

"I know, Father."

"I thought I knew what was best for you, for this family. For the baby. We will find some way to live without selling any of our land. I know we will." He set his gaze upon the fire, looking into it as though the flames would speak. "I only hope he does not do or say anything to sully your reputation. It is not truly my wish for you to remain a spinster. And if your actions regarding Henry Hanover are any indication, you do not wish that for yourself."

Henry Hanover! How she wished she had never heard the name!

The truth of Father's statements showed Abigail that her rejection of Cecil bore real consequences. Her heart beat with newfound fear. What if Cecil went home and told Tedric that she was a loathsome, ill-mannered creature? What if Cecil demanded that Tedric never see Abigail again?

seventeen

Tedric waited with a sense of anticipation, wistfulness, and dread. In times such as these, he reached for his Bible. Tonight the darkness forbade it. All he could do was to wait in the carriage. Wind whistled past outside. He shivered, grateful that at least he was sheltered from the night air.

He wondered what was happening inside the Pettigrew manor house. Surely by this time, they were all celebrating. Then again, wouldn't they have invited him in to share in the joy?

Tedric's thoughts concentrated on Abigail and Cecil's betrothal. He imagined the nuptials would take place in the autumn, with the leaves at peak color. He pictured himself standing beside his brother, watching him take the wedding vows that he should be taking. He would watch helplessly as his brother kissed his new bride.

Tedric bristled. He tried to peer into the windows of the house, but he couldn't see anything through the closed draperies. If only Abigail could break away long enough to tell him what was transpiring!

No. He couldn't think of Abigail any longer. Tedric had kept his thoughts to himself as much as he could when Cecil had confronted him, but he feared the expression on his face revealed more than he intended. Did everyone, including his future sister-in-law, know he loved Abigail?

He groaned.

Father in heaven, I beg of You, give me strength!

At that moment, Tedric heard Cecil's footfalls as he made his way toward the carriage. Just outside, he heard Cecil instruct the driver to take them home. The door creaked open, and Cecil entered the carriage. He took the seat beside Tedric.

"What happened?" Tedric was aware of the pleading tone his voice conveyed.

"We can discuss that when we arrive home."

Why did Cecil's tone sound ominous, somehow?

Minutes ticked by as they rode in silence. Unable to discern anything from Cecil's expression, Tedric speculated about what Cecil would tell him once they were alone. He prayed that the news wouldn't devastate both families.

"Let us go to the library," Cecil suggested as they disembarked in front of the house. "The fire should still be warm there."

Tedric nodded. His stomach knotted. He hurried to the library, but not before Cecil could instruct the maid to bring him a glass of port. As soon as the brothers entered the room, they sat in opposite chairs in front of the fireplace. Though dying, the embers still emitted a degree of warmth.

"I want to know what happened," Tedric said. "You hardly seem like a man looking forward to his wedding day."

"That is because I am not such a man," Cecil answered. "The betrothal is off."

"Off?" Tedric paused. He had to let the news register. "I do not believe it. Pettigrew would never risk the legal repercussions of breaking a contract with a Sutton."

"He did not break it. I did."

"You must be daft," Tedric said.

"Crazy? Perhaps."

"Why did you do it?" Tedric wondered.

"You are no small part of the reason, brother dear." Cecil leaned toward him. "Why did you not tell me that the little miss had fallen in love with you?"

Spasms erupted in Tedric's stomach as his emotions roiled. "What did she say after I left?"

"Nothing. She did not need to say a word. And neither did you. You allowed me to go over there and make a fool of myself. I hope you had a good laugh." Cecil snapped. He leaned back and folded his arms over his fleshy chest.

"On the contrary, I find nothing humorous about my brother being made to appear foolish in front of others," Tedric said. "But if I may be permitted to say so, brother dear, you are a fool."

"What is that?" Cecil's eyes narrowed.

"Just because Abigail misunderstood and thought herself in love with me does not mean you should not marry her."

The maid interrupted. "Your wine, M'lord." She handed him a glass of port containing a great deal more liquid than was customary for most gentlemen to consume in one sitting.

"Thank you. And tell Mrs. Farnsworth that we need more logs on this fire."

"Yes, M'lord."

Cecil held his glass up to the light of the fire. "At least here we have the proper vintage. The Pettigrew stock is quite inadequate."

"That should be of no surprise to you. Of course they do not have our resources—or your keen interest in wine," Tedric couldn't resist adding.

Cecil took a swig and lifted his glass. "A fine vintage. Worth waiting for." He narrowed his eyes at Tedric. "Not unlike waiting for your Miss Pettigrew?"

"My Miss Pettigrew? No, Cecil. I never did anything the least bit improper with her. She is your betrothed, not mine."

"Was my betrothed."

"I am hoping you will come to your senses and beg Pettigrew to keep the contract intact. If you perceive any threat from me, then you are mistaken," Tedric assured him. "I plan to move to London after the wedding." Even as he made the promise, Tedric clenched his teeth in regret.

"So I was right about that look in your eyes," Cecil said. "You are in love with her."

"I said no such thing."

"You would not be planning to move if you were not afraid of being in the same house with her."

"I am not afraid," Tedric protested. " I–I just—"

Cecil laughed. "Spoken like a befuddled, besotted man so deep in love he is likely to drown in it."

Though not prone to blushing, Tedric felt his face flush hot. He was nevertheless determined not to look as silly as a schoolgirl. He stared into his brother's eyes.

"I see you are unable to deny it." A sly smile crossed Cecil's lips. "Never mind. I rather enjoy your discomfort. You certainly have seen me in unflattering states often enough. It is about time the tables were turned." Cecil chuckled and then took another swallow of port. "Just realize here and now that you will not be moving."

"I beg your pardon?"

"You heard me," Cecil said. "You will stay right here at the estate. And if you know what is good for you, you will marry Miss Abigail Pettigrew."

Tedric's beating heart betrayed him. Could Cecil really mean what he said? "Cecil, you are drunk."

"For once, I am not. I am perfectly sober." He downed the rest of his drink as though the action would prove his point. "I must say I was rather surprised by Miss Pettigrew."

"Surprised?"

"Yes. Due to her young age, I was expecting a meek, mousy little thing." Cecil poured himself another glass of port. "I found her to be pleasant enough in appearance, though her temperament was more fiery than I expected."

Tedric smiled. "You have described her well."

Cecil didn't return his smile. "I am almost sorry she came to mistake you for her betrothed."

"For that, I do beg your forgiveness once again. Surely you realize I never meant—"

Cecil shook his hand at Tedric as he always did when he was annoyed with his little brother. "Yes, yes. I know. You are too much of a prig to try to steal her away intentionally."

Tedric felt his lips tighten. Cecil's habit of labeling him a prig was vexing, but to challenge Cecil at that moment meant he could lose his brother's forgiveness—and Abigail.

"The whole mistake is understandable, really," Cecil babbled. "She doesn't know our family. We were both away at school since she was a child, and Father was a recluse himself after Mama's death."

"You need not tell me," Tedric agreed. "Abigail's presence brought a life to this place I hadn't seen in twenty years." Tedric froze. He had once again said too much. "I beg your pardon—"

"Pardon for what? Complimenting the woman who was to be a member of this family?"

Tedric let out a sigh. "Cecil, you say you are no fool, but in breaking the betrothal you have just relinquished a fine lady. She has a good name, and she is certain to be a fine mother."

"I shall not waste time arguing that point," Cecil answered. "I have no worries. I can easily make other plans. There are more ladies in need of a husband than there are eligible eldest sons, you know." He sent Tedric a confident nod.

"I know." Mothers of eligible ladies sought Cecil's company for their daughters despite his lack of character.

"I have at least two promising prospects among the ladies of my acquaintance in London." Cecil puffed out his chest with pride and then gulped more port.

Tedric recalled one brassy lass in particular. "I know you have no need of money, but please do not tell me you mean to marry Lizzie."

"Oh, no." Cecil threw back his head and laughed. "I may be a rogue, but I am not a madman. Lizzie and I will always enjoy each other's company. My future wife will know about our little arrangement, and she shall turn a blind eye." Cecil stared into the fire. His voice became distant. "I am not sure that Miss Pettigrew, with her obvious idealism and youth, would be so willing."

The thought that Abigail, a woman certain to devote her heart to the man she married, would be treated with such utter disrespect, sent ire through Tedric's being. "I doubt it," he answered. "She is devout."

Cecil returned his full attention to his brother. "Then I should say she is a perfect match for you, Tedric."

A perfect match! So even Cecil could see that Abigail was the answer to Tedric's many hours of prayer. Still, he hesitated. "I cannot take her, Cecil, even if she would have me. I must remember our family honor."

"Family honor? Ha! I have ruined our family honor for years, and I am still the most sought-after bachelor in the parish." Cecil leaned over and patted him on the knee. "Tedric, you know firsthand that I have not led what most people would think is a very good life. I have enjoyed my pleasures far away in the city while leaving you here to tend to the estate. I have broken a few hearts and wasted a fortune along the way."

"It is not too late, you know. If you approach God with sincere prayer and a repentant heart, He will forgive you everything. He will give you a new life, a life much more fulfilling than anything you have ever known or can ever imagine."

"Really?" Cecil shook his head. "I believe I still have plenty of time to be good. Sometime, when I am old and gray and have grandchildren running about and sitting on my knee, that is the time I will be ready to be good."

"Mother forced you to attend worship services enough to remember what Proverbs says," Tedric reminded his brother. " 'Boast not thyself of tomorrow; for thou knowest not what a day may bring forth.' "

"Committing Scripture to memory was never my strong suit as it is yours, brother dear."

Cecil's voice was reprimanding enough to bring to an end Tedric's speech. Helpless to stop his brother, Tedric watched him finish a second glass of port.

"As you can see, at this moment I am enjoying myself. In the meantime," said Cecil, "God and I have an understanding. So do not worry about my mortal soul. I am sure God has better things for you to do than to vex yourself over me."

"But I do," Tedric said. "I pray for you each day."

"I suppose I should thank you for that." Cecil sent Tedric a bittersweet smile. "In return, will you let me do one good thing for you? Will you let me do one unselfish thing in my life?" He paused. "Please, go over to the Pettigrews' tomorrow. Ask Abigail to be your wife."

"My wife?" The thought was too delicious!

"Yes."

Tedric's emotions crashed to the ground. "But I cannot offer her a title or the estate."

"She does not impress me as one who is concerned about titles. As for the estate. . ." Cecil shrugged. "You can live here as long as you like. In fact, I want you to live here."

"But as the second son, that is not my right."

"The privilege is not without obligation," Cecil said. "I expect you to continue to care for the estate and bring it back to its former glory. I do wish you to keep my bedchamber in the south wing ready for me when I care to return to the country to hunt."

Tedric thought for a moment. "I see no reason why that would not be agreeable."

"I am sure, especially since you shall not see much of me. You are perfectly aware that I much prefer to live most of the year in London. And as for income, you have Mother's money."

Calculations flew through Tedric's brain. "Yes," he answered. "I suppose I do have a reasonably secure life to offer her."

"Do not delay," Cecil urged. "It is well before bedtime. Send a message to her father that you will be seeing him on the morrow to ask for Miss Pettigrew's hand in marriage."

Marriage! Tedric swallowed.

"If you act quickly, Pettigrew may even send you an answer tonight."

"Tonight." Tedric noticed his palms had become sweaty with high anticipation. "Are you sure? Are you perfectly sure?"

"Yes, I am sure. I have never been as certain of anything in my life."

eighteen

The following day, Abigail heard a knock on her bedroom door as she dressed for the morning.

"Come in, Missy."

The events of the previous night had left Abigail wrestling with her thoughts and feelings, and sleep had eluded her. Last evening, in the space of a half hour, she had journeyed from believing she would marry the love of her life to suffering a broken betrothal with a man she had never wanted. She had been confident of her future the night before, but in the light of day, uncertainty clutched at her.

The exchange between Father and Cecil had served only to deepen her depression. She wondered what had transpired between the brothers at the Sutton estate after the fateful meeting. Abigail was certain that Cecil had portrayed her father to Tedric as a dishonorable deceiver. Tedric would most likely avoid her at all costs now!

Her aching heart betrayed her with its constant yearning. How could she have let herself fall in love with Tedric? If she had known he could never be hers, Abigail would have kept her feelings at bay. Now it was too late. She gave her sleeve an angry yank as she pulled it onto her shoulder.

She sighed. What good would ripping her dress do? She had no right to believe she should escape the consequences of her foolish actions.

Heavenly Father, deliver me from this torment of doubt!

"Mornin', M'lady," Missy said.

Abigail startled and then spun around to face the maid.

"I beg pardon, M'lady. I didn't mean to scare ye none." Missy curtsied.

"That is quite all right," Abigail assured her.

Abigail rued the day when Missy would leave. Since the betrothal was broken, the Suttons were bound to send for their maid soon. She tried not to look at Missy for fear emotion would overtake her.

Abigail summoned her most cheerful voice. "I have been waiting for you. Here." She turned her back to the maid. "I need help with these buttons."

"I'll help ye, M'lady." She felt Missy's hands come into contact with a button and pull the opposing cotton toward it. "But are ye sure ye want to be wearin' such a plain house dress to see yer beloved?"

"My beloved?" She swirled to meet Missy's eyes, which were fixed on her. "I have no beloved. Not after last night. Please, should anyone call today, tell him I am not at home."

"I don't understand, M'lady."

"I do." Griselda's voice sounded from the entrance. "I thought you would say something so foolish."

"Good morning," Abigail blurted out of years of forced habit.

"Good morning." Griselda's footfalls, slow and uneven with her waddling, approached until she stood before Abigail.

"I am not being foolish," Abigail protested.

"I beg to differ." Griselda investigated Abigail's gray dress. She tilted her head toward Missy. "You. Dress her in the garment she wore last night. And style her hair."

Missy stopped buttoning the dress. Frozen in motion, the maid obviously awaited Abigail's approval.

"No, Griselda," said Abigail. "Did you not hear what I said? I am not at home for callers today."

"Do as I say, Missy," Griselda commanded.

"Yes, Ma'am." Missy curtsied and hurried to the wardrobe to retrieve the dress in question.

"Now that I think about it, I suppose you might have a good idea," Abigail noted. "Perhaps if Lord Sutton sees me in the same dress, he will assume we are even poorer than he thought. Perhaps he will take pity on me and spare me the lecture.

Perhaps he might even decide to marry me after all."

"Do you think I am ignorant of last evening's events?" Griselda asked. "I spoke with your father. He related the entire episode."

"Then you know very well that I have no beloved."

"Au contraire. I believe you do." Griselda arched an eyebrow. "I understand that Tedric Sutton's name was mentioned."

Upon the utterance of Tedric's name, Abigail's stomach felt as though it were leaping to the base of her throat. "And what does it matter if his name was mentioned?" she managed to ask.

"You were mistaken in your assumption that Lord Sutton is here to see you. Your visitor is not he, but Tedric Sutton."

"Here? Where?" Abigail rushed to look out of her window.

"In the parlor," Griselda informed her. "He is waiting to see you."

She turned and faced her stepmother. "I do not want to see him. Send him away," Abigail spat out.

"I beg to differ," Griselda answered. "I think you want to see him very badly."

"What does it matter? Father would never approve. Not after last night. Lord Sutton all but called Father a liar to his face."

"Are you really willing to hold Tedric responsible for Lord Sutton's words and actions?" Griselda wondered.

"Are you forgetting that they are both of the same family?" An unpleasant thought occurred to Abigail, stabbing through her being. "Perhaps Tedric is here to admonish me further for the way I treated his brother."

"Nonsense."

"How do you know?" Abigail queried.

Griselda paused. "A woman can tell by the look in a man's eyes."

Abigail remembered the look she once thought she had seen in Henry Hanover's eyes. She had long since realized that his way of surveying her was nothing more than lust.

How she had misconstrued his intentions!

Her thoughts moved to Tedric. His eyes never bespoke an unsavory love or hinted at any impropriety. Abigail had no brother, but examination of Tedric's actions toward her could only point to the fact that he thought of her as nothing more than a future family relation. Had that connection not been anticipated, Tedric might well have left her on the road that night. No wonder he had acted with such disdain when she gave him the gifts. No wonder he had never tried to hold her, even to kiss her cheek. . . .

"Tedric Sutton awaits," Griselda reminded her.

"I wonder what he wants?" Abigail's heart beat with a mixture of curiosity, fear, and anticipation. "Maybe I should tell him to go away. Perhaps see him another time."

"I do not advise that. I happen to know that the Suttons' messenger arrived late last night with a letter for your father. I did not have the privilege of reading it, but I wonder if that letter was from Tedric, asking your father for your hand."

Abigail felt her blood race with excitement. Then a horrible thought occurred to her. "Or the messenger may have been delivering a letter from Lord Sutton to break off the betrothal formally," she countered. "Where is Father? I want to ask him about the letter."

"He has gone into the village. I suspect he did not anticipate you would be receiving a caller this early in the morning. Despite the early hour, you must see him. If you do not, he may never come back." Griselda's gray eyes looked into Abigail's.

"Tedric was never mine," Abigail whispered.

"I believe he is now, if you want him to be. He loves you."

"What do you care about love?" Abigail quarreled. "You only wanted me to marry Lord Sutton so I, and consequently you, could gain access to the Sutton fortune. His younger brother stands to gain none of the Sutton holdings. So what would a marriage to Tedric offer you?"

Griselda's neck whipped ever so slightly toward the fire and back, as though Abigail had taken her hand and slapped her across the cheek. "Have we not progressed in the least, Abigail? Have you not developed the least bit of affection for me during your time here?"

Abigail let her gaze drop to the floor. She searched her heart before she answered. "Yes." She lifted her face toward Griselda. "Yes I have. More affection than I ever thought possible."

"And I, you. Go to him, Abigail. Do not worry about the consequences of money. God will provide for us."

"Do you truly believe that?"

"Now that I have been delving into the Word with you, I believe it. 'Are not two sparrows sold for a farthing? and one of them shall not fall on the ground without your Father. But the very hairs of your head are all numbered. Fear ye not therefore, ye are of more value than many sparrows.' " Griselda sent her a smile no less triumphant than that of an eager pupil looking for the approval of a stern governess. "Matthew chapter ten, verses twenty-nine through thirty-one," she cited.

"Yes, that is one of my favorite passages as well."

"So you see," Griselda said, "even if you only meet with Tedric to tell him you never want to speak to him again, you should give him the courtesy of listening to what he has to say."

"Well. . ." Abigail hesitated.

"Remember, you are a Pettigrew. Appearances are everything."

"All right. I shall go."

"Good," Griselda said. "Now, will you allow Missy to prepare you for your meeting? I am perfectly willing to send the maid out with a round of tea and biscuits for your guest to consume as he waits."

"I hope my toilette shall not take quite that long."

Griselda exited, a knowing smile covering her face.

"Are ye ready to dress proper?" Missy asked.

Abigail nodded. "I am ready."

Since Missy had become more adept at styling her hair,

Abigail was ready only a few minutes later. Slowly, she donned the rose-colored dress, making sure the lace curved about her neck to conceal any immodest flesh. If this meeting would truly be her last with Tedric, she wanted him to remember her at her most beautiful.

"Ye never looked lovelier, M'lady," Missy assured her.

"I hope you are right. Perhaps he will be less harsh with me if my appearance is pleasant."

"Harsh? With the woman he wants to marry?"

"No matter what my stepmother says, I have no idea he plans to propose," Abigail said. "He may be here to say he is moving away, that he will never see me again. But not before he lashes out at me about being so foolish." Abigail felt a mist of tears threaten.

"There, there. It shan't be so bad. Now don't ye start with yer cryin'. Ye go down there and face him like the lady ye are."

Abigail nodded. Missy was right. After summoning her courage, Abigail descended the stairs, made her way through the foyer, and stopped in front of the parlor entrance. As soon as she was announced, she crossed the threshold to face Tedric.

Tedric had risen from his seat and was standing to his full height. He cut an unusually striking figure in his form-fitting morning suit. Hat removed, Tedric's hair shone in the morning sunbeams that streamed in a thin line through a crack in the draperies. She looked beside the chair for his riding whip. If she saw it, she knew it to be a signal that the visit would be short. When she didn't spot the whip, Abigail wasn't sure whether his failure to bring it in was a good sign or bad. If he planned to linger, he must be prepared to give her quite a lecture. Then again, the half-eaten plate of biscuits and pot of tea indicated his acceptance of their hospitality.

"Abigail." His voice was soft, softer than she expected, with a quality that both excited and reassured her.

"Tedric."

His eyes held an eager light. Could he hear her beating heart? He strode toward her and reached for her hand, but not before looking into her eyes to seek her silent permission. After she gave him one nod, he took her hand in his. Tedric lifted it to his lips and barely brushed her hand against them.

Abigail wasn't sure how to respond. She had expected him to shout, to make accusations, but never this. Perhaps he displayed gallantry to throw her off balance. After revealing all of her feelings for him on the previous night, she braced herself for a lecture on how much she embarrassed him and how a proper lady should behave.

"Abigail, I have so much to say to you. Where do I begin?"

"Perhaps with the letter. The letter that I understand arrived here in the dead of night."

"You do not know its contents?" he asked.

"No. Father is in the village, and I did not know until this morning that your messenger had delivered a letter here. I have not seen Father today. You do know the hour is early for callers."

"I beg your indulgence." His voice was soft, but she didn't want to fall into a trap.

"Very well. Please tell me why you have come here," she answered, though her voice remained soft. "I am certain I deserve anything you have to say to me."

His eyes widened. "You seem not to believe I bear good tidings."

"Should I?" She bowed her head. "Last evening, I know my actions did not prove the good breeding that I claim is mine."

"You acted like a perfect lady," Tedric said. "A lady who was shocked by unexpected developments and a victim of a misunderstanding."

His words gave her hope. She looked up into his face. "Nevertheless, I beg your forgiveness for my display."

"I am the one who should be begging your forgiveness. I am afraid I did not defend your honor with the vehemence that I should have. Rather, I permitted you to defend me. But I had good reason. As much as it hurt my heart, I did not want to risk saying anything that would jeopardize your betrothal to my brother. No matter how he praises the ladies in London, no one could match you." Tedric took both of her hands in his. "I am sorry about what happened here last night. I am at fault for my brother's decision to break off the betrothal."

"So you have come here to beg my forgiveness rather than to lecture and to blame me?"

"I blame you for nothing."

"And I do not hold you to any blame." She looked down at the floor. "Except that, why did you not tell me?"

"Tell you what? That Cecil was your betrothed? I thought you knew. That is why I never—"

"Never what?" She gazed into his blue eyes.

"Never—oh, Abigail, how I wanted to tell you for so long, but I could not until now. I love you. I always have, from the first moment we met. And I love you even more today."

She gave his hands a gentle squeeze. "And I love you, Tedric. Desperately. You have no notion of how long I have waited for you to say those words."

"The day you gave me the gifts. . ."

"Yes," she whispered.

"I thought I saw love in your eyes. How I hated to disappoint you by not expressing the depth of my emotion. Even worse, I hated myself for loving you! But now—"

"Now you do not have to hate yourself anymore. Oh, Tedric. I had no idea I had caused you such pain!"

"But not of your own accord, my dearest. All along, I was causing you hurt, though doing so broke my own heart. Knowing you were my brother's betrothed prevented me from showing my true feelings toward you," Tedric answered. "I understand everything now. The fact that you respect my brother so much that you would honor your engagement to him even when you in fact loved me makes me love you all the more."

Abigail had a terrible thought. "I have to know. Does he mind terribly? I am afraid I was quite rude to him."

"He knows you were surprised. How else could you have reacted?"

"More like a lady, I suppose. I all but threw him out of the house in favor of you," Abigail reminded him.

"I must admit, I have never seen my peppery little Abigail so beautiful."

"Peppery!" She gasped, remembering the first day they had met, the day when he had ridden up on his horse and teased her with his bold description of her. "Peppery!"

He let out a hearty chuckle. "That is my Abigail. The one I first met. I am afraid I must take back my earlier comment that you were never more beautiful than last night. I do believe you are even more ravishing today."

"I am? Even though I did not heed your warning?"

"What warning?" he asked.

"That first day we met," she recalled. "You warned me not to stay too close to the road lest I be swept away."

Remembrance made his handsome face shine. "Oh, yes. That warning."

"I am afraid I did stray too close to the road, and I was swept away, just as you predicted." She gave his hands a squeeze. "I was swept away by the man who proved to be a light among shadows. The man I grew to love. If there was any doubt before, let there be no doubt now."

"And I, you." He gazed into her face. "Yes, even Cecil knows it. He practically commanded me to ask you to marry me."

At that moment, she wondered if her knees would give way. But if they did, she knew Tedric would rescue her, just as he had done that night in the churchyard. "Do you really mean it?"

"Yes. I followed Cecil's advice and sent the letter right away. Your father has already granted his permission." Tedric paused. "I–I believe he now realizes how much I love you."

"Yes, I think he does."

Without another moment's hesitation, Tedric touched one knee to the floor. "Will you, Abigail? Will you be my wife?"

She didn't need to take time to consider. "Yes! Yes! A thousand times, yes!"

Tedric rose and embraced her. "You have made me the happiest I have ever been in my life."

"As you have me, my beloved." She broke the embrace, but only because her desire to look into his eyes overwhelmed her. "My beloved! How wonderful it feels to call you that after thinking of you in that way for so long."

"May I?" He leaned toward her and took her once again in his arms. The reasons to resist existed no longer. His lips drew close to hers in anticipation of a kiss.

"Always," she answered, her heart beating against his chest. "Now and forever more."

epilogue

"Mirabelle is so beautiful, Griselda." Abigail sighed as she watched the little girl crawl through the grass in the side yard of the Pettigrew manor house. Mirabelle's dark curls reminded her of Griselda's.

"If you had told me two years ago that Griselda would ask me to give our child your middle name, Abigail, I never would have believed it," Father told them.

"What do you think we should name our little girl, Abigail, now that such a beautiful name is taken?" Tedric asked.

"I am certain that God will grant you many children, so you will have the opportunity to bestow upon them many names," Father said.

"That is your hope, is it not, Father?"

"Of course. What man would not be blessed to know many grandchildren?"

"Perhaps we should name a little girl Griselda," Tedric suggested.

"Or we could start a new tradition," Griselda suggested. "You could use my middle name of Diane."

"Indeed." Tedric wasn't looking at Griselda, but at his wife. He swept his hand over Abigail's cheek. She felt the same little thrill now that she had on their wedding day. Only now, they were even closer as man and wife.

"What is all this talk about little girls? Wishful thinking?" Father's eyes twinkled.

"Not anymore, Father." Unwilling to broach such a delicate topic further, Abigail merely concentrated on watching little Mirabelle.

Father and Griselda gasped at once.

"How wonderful!" Griselda congratulated her. She leaned

over and gave Abigail's hand a squeeze.

"Indeed!" Father shook Tedric's hand. "Naturally, one must be prepared for a little boy."

"If God grants us a boy, he shall be named after you, Father," Abigail said.

They heard the clapping of little hands. Mirabelle obviously approved.

Tedric and Abigail exchanged a knowing glance, one in which they promised each other a lifetime of dreams fulfilled.

A Letter To Our Readers

ear Reader:

In order that we might better contribute to your reading oyment, we would appreciate your taking a few minutes to pond to the following questions. We welcome your comnts and read each form and letter we receive. When comted, please return to the following:

Fiction Editor
Heartsong Presents
PO Box 719
Uhrichsville, Ohio 44683

Did you enjoy reading *A Light among Shadows* by Tamela ncock Murray?

❑ Very much! I would like to see more books by this author!

❑ Moderately. I would have enjoyed it more if

____

____

____

Are you a member of **Heartsong Presents**? ❑ Yes ❑ No
If no, where did you purchase this book?________________

____

How would you rate, on a scale from 1 (poor) to 5 (superior), the cover design? ________________________

On a scale from 1 (poor) to 10 (superior), please rate the following elements.

____ Heroine
____ Hero
____ Setting
____ Plot
____ Inspirational theme
____ Secondary characters

5. These characters were special because?________________

____

____

6. How has this book inspired your life?________________

____

____

7. What settings would you like to see covered in future **Heartsong Presents** books? ________________

____

____

8. What are some inspirational themes you would like to see treated in future books? ________________

____

____

9. Would you be interested in reading other **Heartsong Presents** titles? ❑ Yes ❑ No

10. Please check your age range:

❑ Under 18	❑ 18-24
❑ 25-34	❑ 35-45
❑ 46-55	❑ Over 55

Name____

Occupation ___________________________________

Address______________________________________

City__________________ State________ Zip__________

Texas Belles

In the Wild West town of Springton, certain Texas belles are finding rattlesnakes easier to lasso than the hearts of the men they desire.

Follow the romantic exploits and spiritual journeys of Springton's finest—as well as a couple of her less-than-upstanding citizens—and watch God's love unfold in each life.

Historical, paperback, 364 pages, 5 3/16" x 8"

Please send me ____ copies of *Texas Belles.* I am enclosing $6.97 for each. (Please add $2.00 to cover postage and handling per order. OH add 6% tax.)

Send check or money order, no cash or C.O.D.s please.

Name ______________________________

Address ______________________________

City, State, Zip ______________________________

To place a credit card order, call 1-800-847-8270.

Send to: Heartsong Presents Reader Service, PO Box 721, Uhrichsville, OH 44683

Heartsong

HISTORICAL ROMANCE IS CHEAPER BY THE DOZEN!

Buy any assortment of twelve *Heartsong Presents* titles and save 25% off of the already discounted price of $3.25 each!

*plus $2.00 shipping and handling per order and sales tax where applicable.

HEARTSONG PRESENTS TITLES AVAILABLE NOW:

__HP179 *Her Father's Love,* N. Lavo
__HP180 *Friend of a Friend,* J. Richardson
__HP183 *A New Love,* V. Wiggins
__HP184 *The Hope That Sings,* J. A. Grote
__HP195 *Come Away My Love,* T. Peterson
__HP203 *Ample Portions,* D. L. Christner
__HP208 *Love's Tender Path,* B. L. Etchison
__HP212 *Crosswinds,* S. Rohde
__HP215 *Tulsa Trespass,* N. J. Lutz
__HP216 *Black Hawk's Feather,* C. Scheidies
__HP219 *A Heart for Home,* N. Morris
__HP223 *Threads of Love,* J. M. Miller
__HP224 *Edge of Destiny,* D. Mindrup
__HP227 *Bridget's Bargain,* L. Lough
__HP228 *Falling Water Valley,* M. L. Colln
__HP235 *The Lady Rose,* J. Williams
__HP236 *Valiant Heart,* S. Laity
__HP239 *Logan's Lady,* T. Peterson
__HP240 *The Sun Still Shines,* L. Ford
__HP243 *The Rising Son,* D. Mindrup
__HP247 *Strong as the Redwood,* K. Billerbeck
__HP248 *Return to Tulsa,* N. J. Lutz
__HP259 *Five Geese Flying,* T. Peterson
__HP260 *The Will and the Way,* D. Pace
__HP263 *The Starfire Quilt,* A. Allen
__HP264 *Journey Toward Home,* C. Cox
__HP271 *Where Leads the Heart,* C. Coble
__HP272 *Albert's Destiny,* B. L. Etchision
__HP275 *Along Unfamiliar Paths,* A. Rognlie
__HP279 *An Unexpected Love,* A. Boeshaar
__HP299 *Em's Only Chance,* R. Dow
__HP300 *Changes of the Heart,* J. M. Miller
__HP303 *Maid of Honor,* C. R. Scheidies
__HP304 *Song of the Cimarron,* K. Stevens
__HP307 *Silent Stranger,* P. Darty
__HP308 *A Different Kind of Heaven,* T. Shuttlesworth
__HP319 *Margaret's Quest,* M. Chapman
__HP320 *Hope in the Great Southland,* M. Hawkins
__HP323 *No More Sea,* G. Brandt
__HP324 *Love in the Great Southland,* M. Hawkins
__HP327 *Plains of Promise,* C. Coble
__HP331 *A Man for Libby,* J. A. Grote
__HP332 *Hidden Trails,* J. B. Schneider
__HP339 *Birdsong Road,* M. L. Colln
__HP340 *Lone Wolf,* L. Lough
__HP343 *Texas Rose,* D. W. Smith
__HP344 *The Measure of a Man,* C. Cox
__HP351 *Courtin' Patience,* K. Comeaux
__HP352 *After the Flowers Fade,* A. Rognlie
__HP356 *Texas Lady,* D. W. Smith
__HP363 *Rebellious Heart,* R. Druten
__HP371 *Storm,* D. L. Christner
__HP372 *'Til We Meet Again,* P. Griffin
__HP380 *Neither Bond Nor Free,* N. C. Pykare
__HP384 *Texas Angel,* D. W. Smith
__HP387 *Grant Me Mercy,* J. Stengl
__HP388 *Lessons in Love,* N. Lavo
__HP392 *Healing Sarah's Heart,* T. Shuttlesworth
__HP395 *To Love a Stranger,* C. Coble
__HP400 *Susannah's Secret,* K. Comeaux
__HP403 *The Best Laid Plans,* C. M. Parker
__HP407 *Sleigh Bells,* J. M. Miller
__HP408 *Destinations,* T. H. Murray
__HP411 *Spirit of the Eagle,* G. Fields
__HP412 *To See His Way,* K. Paul
__HP415 *Sonoran Sunrise,* N. J. Farrier
__HP416 *Both Sides of the Easel,* B. Youree
__HP419 *Captive Heart,* D. Mindrup
__HP420 *In the Secret Place,* P. Griffin
__HP423 *Remnant of Forgiveness,* S. Laity
__HP424 *Darling Cassidy,* T. V. Bateman
__HP427 *Remnant of Grace,* S. K. Downs
__HP428 *An Unmasked Heart,* A. Boeshaar

(If ordering from this page, please remember to include it with the order form.)

Presents

- __HP431 *Myles from Anywhere,* J. Stengl
- __HP432 *Tears in a Bottle,* G. Fields
- __HP435 *Circle of Vengeance,* M. J. Conner
- __HP436 *Marty's Ride,* M. Davis
- __HP439 *One With the Wind,* K. Stevens
- __HP440 *The Stranger's Kiss,* Y. Lehman
- __HP443 *Lizzy's Hope,* L. A. Coleman
- __HP444 *The Prodigal's Welcome,* K. Billerbeck
- __HP447 *Viking Pride,* D. Mindrup
- __HP448 *Chastity's Angel,* L. Ford
- __HP451 *Southern Treasures,* L. A. Coleman
- __HP452 *Season of Hope,* C. Cox
- __HP455 *My Beloved Waits,* P. Darty
- __HP456 *The Cattle Baron's Bride,* C. Coble
- __HP459 *Remnant of Light,* T. James
- __HP460 *Sweet Spring,* M. H. Flinkman
- __HP463 *Crane's Bride,* L. Ford
- __HP464 *The Train Stops Here,* G. Sattler
- __HP467 *Hidden Treasures,* J. Odell
- __HP468 *Tarah's Lessons,* T. V. Bateman
- __HP471 *One Man's Honor,* L. A. Coleman
- __HP472 *The Sheriff and the Outlaw,* K. Comeaux
- __HP475 *Bittersweet Bride,* D. Hunter
- __HP476 *Hold on My Heart,* J. A. Grote
- __HP479 *Cross My Heart,* C. Cox
- __HP480 *Sonoran Star,* N. J. Farrier
- __HP483 *Forever Is Not Long Enough,* B. Youree
- __HP484 *The Heart Knows,* E. Bonner
- __HP488 *Sonoran Sweetheart,* N. J. Farrier
- __HP491 *An Unexpected Surprise,* R. Dow
- __HP492 *The Other Brother,* L. N. Dooley
- __HP495 *With Healing in His Wings,* S. Krueger
- __HP496 *Meet Me with a Promise,* J. A. Grote
- __HP499 *Her Name Was Rebekah,* B. K. Graham
- __HP500 *Great Southland Gold,* M. Hawkins
- __HP503 *Sonoran Secret,* N. J. Farrier
- __HP504 *Mail-Order Husband,* D. Mills
- __HP507 *Trunk of Surprises,* D. Hunt
- __HP508 *Dark Side of the Sun,* R. Druten
- __HP511 *To Walk in Sunshine,* S. Laity
- __HP512 *Precious Burdens,* C. M. Hake
- __HP515 *Love Almost Lost,* I. B. Brand
- __HP516 *Lucy's Quilt,* J. Livingston
- __HP519 *Red River Bride,* C. Coble
- __HP520 *The Flame Within,* P. Griffin
- __HP523 *Raining Fire,* L. A. Coleman
- __HP524 *Laney's Kiss,* T. V. Bateman
- __HP531 *Lizzie,* L. Ford
- __HP532 *A Promise Made,* J. L. Barton
- __HP535 *Viking Honor,* D. Mindrup
- __HP536 *Emily's Place,* T. Victoria Bateman
- __HP539 *Two Hearts Wait,* F. Chrisman
- __HP540 *Double Exposure,* S. Laity

Great Inspirational Romance at a Great Price!

Heartsong Presents books are inspirational romances in contemporary and historical settings, designed to give you an enjoyable, spirit-lifting reading experience. You can choose wonderfully written titles from some of today's best authors like Peggy Darty, Sally Laity, Tracie Peterson, Colleen L. Reece, Debra White Smith, and many others.

When ordering quantities less than twelve, above titles are $3.25 each. Not all titles may be available at time of order.

SEND TO: **Heartsong Presents** Reader's Service
P.O. Box 721, Uhrichsville, Ohio 44683

Please send me the items checked above. I am enclosing $ ______
(please add $2.00 to cover postage per order. OH add 6.25% tax. NJ add 6%.). Send check or money order, no cash or C.O.D.s, please.

To place a credit card order, call 1-800-847-8270.

NAME ______________________________

ADDRESS ______________________________

CITY/STATE ____________________ ZIP ________

HPS 7-03